HARDNECK
AND AMOS

by

VIC J. HANSON

ROBERT HALE · LONDON

© *Vic J. Hanson 1982*
First published in Great Britain 1982

ISBN 0 7091 9760 8

Robert Hale Limited
Clerkenwell House
Clerkenwell Green
London EC1R 0HT

Photoset by Art Photoset Limited.
Printed in Great Britain by
St. Edmundsbury Press, Bury St. Edmunds, Suffolk.
Bound by Weatherby Woolnough.

PART ONE

New Mexico—Murder

ONE

She was a big woman but shapely, with bright blue eyes and hair like thick, glossy yellow ropes. Her face was plumply fresh and dimpled and when she smiled at passers-by—and maybe called a greeting too—she revealed small, white, and very even teeth. She swung her hips as she walked with her two baskets of produce, one in each hand.

She was moving towards the end of Main Street and there were no other people near when the two men came out of the alley and onto the boardwalk and barred her path.

They had been in the small end-of-town drinking den called The Mexican's and they were both staggering drunk. They had been bemoaning the fact that this town did not have what you could call a regular cathouse and to them now it appeared as if this comely blonde woman had been dropped from the beneficent Heavens, right at their feet, exclusively for them.

They were young and dirty and unshaven and they stank of the rotgut they had been imbibing. The

Mexican's was only patronised by saddle-tramps such as they, regular townsfolk opining that if you drank too much of the kind of concoctions on sale there you were like to go blind. For a moment the two pilgrims might have thought their vision was indeed playing them tricks and, as if to make sure, the taller of the two reached out a skinny arm, saying, "I do purely love big women."

She was already backing, lightly on small feet. The man's long fingers only slightly brushed the cloth which was stretched tightly over the opulence of her breast.

She put both her bags down and straightened herself swiftly from them, her balled fist swinging upwards. It caught the lanky one full in the mouth and he yowled with surprise and pain and staggered backwards. He failed to maintain his already perilous equilibrium and came down hard on his bony rear, the boardwalk shaking beneath him and emitting little puffs of acrid dust.

The second man grabbed for the woman and she swung at him and missed. Part of a disused hitching rail held him up and his companion was holding onto the same piece of timber as he strove to haul himself to his feet.

"Get out of my way, pigs," the woman said.

Her voice was silvery and she had some kind of a foreign accent.

The two men straightened up together, untangling themselves. "I'll get you, you bitch," said the one who had been on the floor.

The woman did not turn and run and the three of them were doing a sort of lopsided square-dance when the two-horse gig came round the bend at the end of Main Street and drew to a halt and the big blackbearded man jumped down.

Both saddle-tramps turned. The bearded man hit the spindle-shanked one with a balled fist that looked like a club, and came down like one too. The thin man went 'Ug' and spiralled into a heap at the foot of the timber that had once been a hitching rack. His companion went for a gun. When Blackbeard picked him up, the man looked momentarily froglike. Then he was thrown headfirst against the nearest wall with a force that made the frame timbers shake. He, also, finished up as a messy sort of heap on the sidewalk.

"You're late, Ad," said the woman accusingly.

"I'm sorry, Oggie," he said in a bass rumble. He jerked a large thumb. "I had to catch Lucy. You know how she hates helpin' to draw the gig."

"You spoil her, that's why."

"Mebbe . . . What was that all about?"

"The poor boys, I think they were drunk."

"Sweepings!" snorted the blackbearded giant. He poked at the recumbent form of the lean man with his foot.

"Oh, Ad, they're alive, aren't they?"

"O' course they are." He inspected them both. "Yeh, they're still breathing."

A tall elderly man came down the street. He had long greying side-burns and a worried expression. He walked as if he had an exposed nail worrying one of his feet and on his breast was a silver star.

"What's going on?" he said querulously.

The big woman told him—while Blackbeard stood by eyeing both of them sardonically.

"Do you want to charge 'em with anything?" the sheriff wanted to know.

"Oh, no," said the woman.

The sheriff turned towards the other man. "Hardneck?"

The giant called Hardneck—or merely 'Ad' by the woman—now said: "Naw. They just need watering well is all."

Both the recumbent men were beginning to groan. The tall lawman took out his gun and prodded both of them in turn with its barrel. "C'mon. On your feet."

"It's surprising how drunks bounce like rubber balls," said Hardneck mildly. "I thought them two would sleep for an hour . . . Howmsoever, we'll be on our way, Ep."

"Mrs Gordino . . . Hardneck."

"Bye, sheriff."

The big man helped his wife and her baskets onto the seat of the gig and perched himself up there also. The equipage looked slightly topheavy as Hardneck turned it and it bowled away.

The sheriff stood scratching his head with his free hand, his gun in his other one as he waited for the two battered drunks to show more animation. He did not look quite so worried now.

Another tall, elderly man came down the street. He was more formally dressed than the sheriff and did not tote a gun in plain sight. He had a big white walrus moustache.

"Howdy, Doc."

"Howdy, Ep. What do we have here?"

"They insulted Mrs Gordino. Then Hardneck happened along."

"They're lucky they aren't in pieces then," the white-moustached doctor said. "Stick 'em in the jail a mite. I'll take a look at 'em'."

"All right." The sheriff moved again.

"That ingrowing toenail still bothering you, Ep?"

"Some."

"I'll take a look at that too."

"Suit yourself."

"Well, if you want it to sort of climb all the way up your leg . . ." The doctor left his sentence unfinished.

The sheriff looked a bit more worried. "Oh, all right, Doc," he said.

The two saddle-tramps were climbing painfully to their feet and looking blearily about them.

"What hit me?" said the smaller one.

"It warn't that big woman, was it?" said the lean one. "Naw, it couldn't be." He looked at the sheriff, the big gun. "We din't mean no harm, suh."

"We'll see about that. March."

One of them limped a whole lot worse than the lawman did. A loafer on a nearby stoop sniggered at the cortège. "Whar's the funeral at?" he wanted to know.

"You can get in the box too, if you like, Barney," barked the sheriff.

"All right, Ep, keep your shirt-tails in." The loafer spat a globule of phlegm into the dust and withdrew through a convenient doorway.

TWO

By the evening Hardneck Gordino was back in the town of Lazy Bend. His wife, Oggie, had prevailed upon him to make a return visit in order to determine that the two saddle-tramps he had punished were not badly hurt.

Hardneck was reluctant to leave her in case the two were not hurt much and had been let loose and planned some sort of retaliation. The Gordinos' little spread was not far from town, easy to find, easy to get to . . .

Oggie said she was not scared of a couple of bruised pilgrims and, anyway, their only hand, old Brackburn would be in his cabin within call and that tough old Indian fighter didn't scare at all.

Hardneck and Brackburn had known each other a long time, off and on, and the old man was as fond of Hardneck's new—and first—wife as he was of the blackbearded giant himself.

Hardneck, riding out on horseback now, gave Brackburn the word. The oldtimer said:

"Don't worry about things here, son. Have yourself a few jars while you're in town. You've been working mighty hard and you need a break."

Sometimes the old man was like a mother hen with two chicks. That was doubtless because Oggie and Hardneck were the only 'family' he had. Brackburn was Hardneck's only 'family' also, apart from Oggie. Her parents, Norwegian immigrants, lived in Philadelphia and she had a brother in Sante Fé.

Hardneck, although he was certainly not your dyed-in-the-wool villain, had been on the owlhoot for a while.* Until, in fact, his partner, one Laughing Luke Benteen had gotten himself killed . . .

Hardneck had functioned for a period after that as a travelling prizefighter, in the bare-knuckle mode. He had met Oggie while she was on her way to visit her brother in Sante Fé. An onlooker would have thought them an ill-assorted pair. But there was something genial and warm about both of them, and they even seemed to think alike. They struck sparks off each other.

They met again by arrangement and the sparks still flew—but always in the most goodnatured way—and they got married.

Old Brackburn had been a rustler as well as an Injun-fighter and he and Hardneck had met from time to time. Then, when Hardneck took up prizefighting, Brackburn became his manager. It had been a comparatively short time, but a congenial one, a *novel* time.

*See 'Muldare'.

During his youth Hardneck had had a legendary tussle with a grizzly bear and had lived to mention it from time to time, though he was an exceedingly modest man. He had scars to prove the truth of the story, however. These were in his neck and they were hideous ones which would have killed a lesser man. For years Hardneck had worn a broad, studded leather collar, hence his nickname.

The leather collar had been great publicity during his prizefighting days—'Hardneck, the man who fought the grizzly'.

Now Hardneck wore a wide silk scarf, and his black beard was protection too. His neck was not nearly so bad as it used to be. Oggie, who had had nursing experience, succoured her man in every way.

They had a nice little spread now. A few prime horses, a parcel of cows. This was good grazing land and the herd was growing and, all being well, they would soon have to take on a couple of extra hands.

As Brackburn had said, Hardneck had been working mighty hard. The older man did his share too, but his younger boss, his old friend, would not let him overdo it, was tough with him about this. And, in this case, Oggie always lent her weight to the argument, on her husband's side. They were big people—and even a big 'softy' like Hardneck could be strong-willed if he felt like it. Brackburn went along, nursed his 'rheumatics'.

In the Autumn of his years he was a happy man and would have given his life for his two friends . . .

So, on that particular night, Hardneck went back to

Lazy Bend . . . Those two drunks had been real hard
nuts. Hardneck had met many such. If Sheriff Ep Leary
still had them, they would not be drunk anymore. But if
not, would Ep have sent them on their way? Suddenly,
Hardneck was anxious to learn what exactly had
happened to the two men who, if sober, might even be
dangerous characters.

He went first to the jail.

"I let 'em out, Hardneck," Ep told him. "You didn't
swear out a complaint. I couldn't do much else. They're
bruised is all. Doc Pierson linimented them. He said
they should get some sleep. They had already got a
room at the hotel. I told 'em to leave town come
morning. We don't want their sort here. I've been
through my dodgers and I haven't got anything on
either of those two characters."

"All right, Ep."

"How's Mrs Hardneck?"

"Oh, she's fine, thanks. It'd take more than two
cruds like those two to faze her."

Ep Leary essayed one of his rare smiles. "Yeh, I
reckon."

As he left the office, Hardneck was much more
relieved in his mind. He decided that, like his old
pardner Brackburn had advised, he would take in a few
drinks. The town was quietish. It was in the main a
hardworking town and this was after-work time and,
for some people, after-supper time.

Hardneck went to the nearest saloon which
happened to be the biggest drinking place in Lazy

Bend, though compared to some of the places Hardneck had seen it was no prize-winner. He sometimes got a yearning for the bright lights, the varieties and fleshpots of places like Tombstone and Abilene, for the long trail, the long loop, the old excitements.

But most times Oggie was exciting enough for him— she was all woman and then some—and, with the work he had been doing lately, he was often too blamed dogtired to think of roaming.

Like the town, the Bide In Saloon was quietish as yet. Hardneck was greeted by a few early topers and by the fat proprietor, whom everybody called Whip but nobody knew why this was so.

Hardneck had a shot of rye with a cold beer chaser, only the beer was not cold. In fact, it was downright warm and the blackbearded man told Whip so. And Whip said:

"The roof has collapsed in my cold cellar, Hardneck, and I can't afford to get it repaired yet. Business is awful, I'll tell you."

"Jumpin' cats," said the blackbearded giant. "I never knew a saloonkeeper who didn't allus claim to be one step from the porehouse."

"It's a fact, Hardneck."

"All right. Mebbe I'll get me a real cold drink down at The Mexican's."

"You can't drink that stuff down there, man. It'll rot your hide."

The big man grinned. "Hell, you know I've got a

copper neck."

Although neither of the two big men knew it at the time, Hardneck was never to reach the drinking den known as The Mexican's.

THREE

Amos Crowle had left the settlement that afternoon after visiting with his old friend Bill Kinnock and Bill's new wife, redheaded Alice.*

The settlement had started as a tent-town but now permanent edifices were rising and it was worthy of being called a town proper, although it didn't have a name yet.

It had been barely twelve months ago that Crowle had been in this territory before. He hadn't expected to be back so soon.

He was glad Bill was finding happiness again though, after going through a tragic patch of time. Bill was settling down. He was no longer for the troubleshooters' trail.

Crowle was trailing a man, a crazy half-breed called Jacel who had violated and killed three women. He had hoped to find Jacel at the settlement, which, in the old

*Alice and Bill featured in a Crowle novel called 'Black Heart's Bunch'—as so did, more briefly, Hardneck Gordino.

days, had been a way-station for all kinds of travellers, the good, the bad and the indifferent. But the settlement was attaining respectability now and nobody had seen no crazy half-Indian.

Not that Jacel looked crazy. He was as cunning as a fox, with a sort of split-nature. He covered his trail well, and now Crowle was beginning to figure that maybe he had lost him.

In the night he saw the lights of what at first he took to be a small town, although he could not remember a town being just here. Maybe, drat it, he had lost his sense of direction!

Or maybe this was another 'settlement' that had sprung up suddenly.

Lights blazed in windows and a yellow wash spilled from open doors and made paths in the darkness. Shining lanterns moved about, obviously carried by people, and as Crowle got nearer, shouting voices were brought to him on the night breeze.

As he got still nearer he saw that the buildings were of wood and looked permanent. This place was certainly not of a temporary sort. But neither was it a town.

This was a ranch, or maybe a small farming co-operative. 'Nesters', as they were called, were getting together now in many parts of the West, joining forces to withstand the intimidations of the big ranchers who wanted the land for themselves and their herds, sometimes huge and wide-ranging. Crowle did not know, however, of a huge ranch in this area and he could not remember having seen this smaller conglomeration before.

He brought his horse to a stop. There seemed to be a lull in the shouting and running-about up ahead there and he wondered if he had been spotted.

He shouted, "Hallo, there, the houses!"

Something buzzed above him and he heard the report of a rifle. In the night it sounded like a distant whiplash.

Feeling very vulnerable, he hunched lower in the saddle. He drew his gun and held it at his side. Maybe he needed his Winchester. But it was in his saddle-boot and he would have to reach further down for it and he didn't want to make any jerky movements.

He shouted, "What in hell's the matter with you people, you crazy or somep'n?"

Now a voice answered him. "Come forward and keep your hands still. There's more than one gun on you."

"All right, I'm coming."

Crowle pouched his Colt again. With a pressure of his knees he started the horse forward again, slowly, easily, though he didn't feel particularly *easy*. He liked to have the initiative and, this time, he had no initiative at all. He had no idea at all about what he was riding into.

They came out to him. They surrounded him and his horse. Half-a-dozen or so of them. Two of them carried lanterns and the rest had guns. There were more guns than cows' ears at a barbecue.

Crowle raised his hands almost to shoulder-level. With the left one he held back his scuffed heavy leather vest so that they could see the badge on his shirt-front. These people, despite their present warlike attitudes, did not seem of the outlaw breed. He said:

"My name is Amos Crowle. I'm in this territory on law business."

"I've heard o' him," said somebody.

"Don't take any chances," said somebody else. "He could've stolen that badge. Maybe he's a friend of the other one."

What other one? thought Crowle. But he did not ask the question. Let these people make the running, damn them—they were beginning to get his goat.

"Take his guns," said another voice.

Crowle did have something to say about that: "Nobody takes my guns." It was a flat unequivocal statement. But he was kind of tired and saddle-sore and he was leaning over backwards to be reasonable. He went on:

"I'll keep my hands up. But nobody takes my guns. Hell, you've got enough fire-power there to start a celebration, with me as the ol' raggedy doll."

They were patently nonplussed—and, momentarily, there was a blank silence. This man did not scare no more than a wildcat in a sheep-pen.

He had a kind of authority about him too, sitting there upright in the saddle, straight, lean, his hands no higher than his shoulders. And he obviously did not mean to lift them any higher.

At length somebody said: "Let's go back. Let him ride ahead."

The man on the horse did not say anything, just kneed his mount gently forward.

The men on foot parted their ranks to let him by and then closed them in behind him; and, led now by the horseman, the cortège approached the lights of the buildings, the carried torches heralding their way.

In a sod yard more people came forth to peer at the prisoner and cluster. Two of them were women. A middle-aged one, an older one. They looked like mother and daughter. The young one appeared scared.

There was an old man there too, and he came closer than anybody, until he was touching the stirrups of the mounted man's horse and looking up at the rider tall in the saddle, an impassive figure.

"Says he's a lawman and that his name's Crowle," said one of the torchbearers.

"That's Amos Crowle all right," said the old man. "I've seed him before."

Crowle was sure he didn't know the old coot from Adam. But, still, that was often the way. He had a certain reputation—he was sardonically aware of that.

Crowle saw that this was his time to take the initiative. "What's been going on here?" he demanded.

A tall man had joined the two women and now said: "Bring him nearer to the house and show him what we've got. Will you get off your horse, suh?"

"Willingly." Crowle got down from the saddle.

They led him forward and there were more torches now, though they were not needed so much. Near the largest building and full in the light streaming from a window lay the body of a man.

The older woman took the younger one into the

house and the door closed behind them.

The tall man said: "He came in the night and tried to molest my daughter and my wife got our loaded shotgun from the wall and gave him both barrels."

Half-breed Jacel was still recognisable, but only just. The buckshot, released at close quarters, had covered a wide area over Jacel's not unhandsome carcase. Jacel had been literally blown into perdition.

"This is the man I was after," Crowle said.

"What was he wanted for?"

"Various things. You name 'em. But lately he murdered three women."

"What shall we do with him?"

"Bury him."

*   *   *

Crowle had coffee, and then he rode on.

He was at a kind of a loose end now, but he hadn't wanted to spend much time with folks he didn't know from a hoot, and who had shot at him too.

He figured that while he was in this territory he would go visit a certain friend. But he would not leave it too late. He didn't aim to get shot at again if he could help it.

He remembered that the town of Lazy Bend was somewhere up ahead. He had been on the right trail all along. It was a pity he had not caught up with that madman Jacel before that young woman got her scare. But she hadn't been hurt none—Momma had taken care of that. Jacel had not deserved to die so quickly.

Crowle figured that the small ranch he now sought was someplace between him and the town and he looked for small lights, no conglomeration like he had come upon before.

The night was dark, with only a sliver of moon. He saw something winking like a star, only it was too low to be a star and there was not another one, not anywhere in the sky.

Presently he halted and called out his nightly greeting: "Halloah, the house."

He saw a figure, and a gruff voice called, "Come on forward, but take it slow."

This was another oldtimer. This one had a shotgun. Another shotgun! Crowle was sick of having guns pointed at him this night. I ought to run the old bastard down, he thought. But he remembered what had happened to Jacel, the way Jacel had looked. It had been a sight to make a man shudder. And he was getting closer all the time.

"Is this Hardneck Gordino's place?" he asked.

"It is." The gruff, elderly-sounding voice was non-committal.

"I thought it was."

"Who are you?"

"My name is Amos Crowle. I'm a friend of Hardneck's. If it comes to that, old hoss, who are you? You weren't here last time I visited."

"I know. I heard about that. I was away visiting my sick sister." The shotgun was dipping lower.

"Did she get well?"

"Hell, yes. She's my older sister. She's ninety-five an' she'll probably outlive me."

A female voice called, "That you, Ad?"

Crowle beat the oldster to the punch. "It's me, Oggie. Amos Crowle."

There was a short silence. Then the silvery female voice said, almost in disbelief. "Amos?"

"Better show yourself," said the old man and he sloped the shotgun over his shoulder and led the way.

Crowle dismounted from his horse, took up the reins again. "C'mon, boy. Chow."

Throwing the words back over his shoulder, the oldster said: "Hardneck went to town and he ain't back yet. He's been gone longer than we expected. That's why we're a mite jumpy, I guess. He had a run-in with a couple of hardcases this afternoon and we're wondering whether he's come up agin 'em tonight as well."

Oggie came forward. "It is you, Amos?"

"I said it was, didn't I? How've you been, Oggie?"

"How've you been?" she mimicked him, her accent more pronounced than usual. Americanese often amused her. "I'm fine. How have you been?"

"Oh, fine, fine. And Hardneck?"

"He's fine too. He is not here at the moment."

"So your friend has just told me. I'll go into Lazy Bend and look for him."

"You will not. You will have some supper. Ad would never forgive me. He can take care of himself, you know that. Perhaps later . . ." She let her voice tail off.

"All right," said Crowle.

FOUR

The drinking den called The Mexican's was in back of some stables and its entrance in an alley. The smell of cheap hooch and greasy food vied with the smell of horses. The hash and booze won—except when the horses were wet. Manure came somewhere down the bottom of the pile.

As Hardneck Gordino passed the open double doors of the stables a light gleamed in its depths and there were the usual rustlings. The old hostler who looked after the stables would be cat-napping in his tiny cubbyhole in the back, but he always came forth with a cheery greeting if travellers turned up. But, for the most part, visiting cowboys who did not live far away left their mounts at one or the other of various hitching racks.

Hardneck turned into the alley. It was dark this end. At the other end only a small shaft of light came through the door which led into The Mexican's, the door—which was usually slightly ajar. It stuck that way and the proprietor—who was not a Mexican—had to put his fat shoulder violently against it in order to shut it each night.

It pulled open easily enough, however—from its ajar position, that is. And now, as Hardneck, coming up the alley, got nearer to the door it literally crashed open.

Two men came out. They turned towards Hardneck and were limned vaguely against the light as they came on—getting further away from the light—and, of course, he could not see their faces.

Behind them there was more light, though it did not illuminate them very much now. A third man came through the door, which must have been left wide open. The light bathed him, but he too was faceless.

Hardneck did not see the gun. He only heard the shots and saw the stabs of flame.

The gunman fired four times. The shots were so close together that they were like a rolling cannonade, filling the alley with noise, the noise rebounding off the wooden walls and making echoes.

Suddenly the men who had been walking were not doing so. One of them was flat on his face and did not seem to be moving. The other one was on all-fours, and he was screaming. The high harsh noise, full of human agony, cut through the gunshot echoes and awakened a banshee ululation. The horrible noise died to a liquid bubbling which then stopped; and then the second man was face down too, beside his still companion.

Hardneck had flattened himself against the wall and drawn his gun. Suddenly his vision was unimpaired by the two men who had been in front of him and he saw the running figure of the killer as the man sped towards the other end of the alley, towards the open spaces.

Hardneck shouted 'Stop!'. He thought right away how silly that was. Maybe the man had not spotted him, and now he had been warned. Hardneck cursed under his breath. He raised his gun to shoulder-height, to arm's length—he tried to draw a bead on the moving figure. In the darkness this was almost an impossibility. He snapped off a shot but did not see the figure falter. Then the man was out of sight around the corner.

Hardneck moved forward. Despite his bulk he was light on his feet and fast.

He paused only momentarily by the two still figures on the ground. He was still shocked by the suddenness of it all. He could not examine the bodies in the gloom and had an idea that it wouldn't be any use anyway. He ran on.

He paused at the corner for only a split moment of time and then he dived out. A slug winged over the top of his head. He hit the ground in a ball and rolled. Another slug kicked up the dirt at his heels.

This second time he had seen the flash of the gun. He rolled over on his belly and lifted his gun and, because of his awkward position, steadied it with his other hand. He squeezed the trigger. Then he rolled again.

The bullet seemed to whine away into nothingness and there was no other sound. The other man did not retaliate. Hardneck could not see him now, did not hear him.

The next sound he heard was one of galloping

hooves. The gunman must have had a horse stashed nearby. The whole thing must have been some sort of a set-up. Hardneck ran in the direction of the sound, which was rapidly diminishing. He thought he saw a swiftly moving shape and he fired his gun again. But the sound of galloping hooves went on and quickly faded and, even as Hardneck turned away, there was a silence except for the soughing of the breeze.

"Hold it right there," a voice called.

Hardneck did not recognise the voice. But he saw the shape, and there were other shapes behind it and more voices, though he could not yet distinguish any more actual words. He shouted, "All right. Take it easy. I'm coming in. That backshooter had a horse stashed. He got away."

"There are a lot of guns pointed at you, mister." It was the same voice again. "Take off your gunbelt and throw it away from you. I want to hear it fall."

"Now wait a minute!"

"Do as I say. Right now. Or we'll start shooting."

"All right, I'm doing it. But you're makin' a mighty big mistake." He heard his gear fall. He was unarmed. He heard another voice and it said:

"I know that goddam rumble. Yeh, I guess . . . That sounds like Hardneck Gordino."

"It is Hardneck," yelled the exasperated giant.

From the back somebody called, "They're both deader'n stinkin' fish. It's them two saddle-tramps the sheriff had in jail for a while."

Somebody else called, "Here *is* the sheriff."

It was late when Amos Crowle got to Lazy Bend. At length Oggie Gordino had been glad to let him go. She was getting really worried about her big husband. Old Brackburn was at hand. The elderly ex-rustler, ex-prizefighter manager and the famous marshal had tacitly accepted each other. One thing Crowle knew for sure was that Oggie was in good hands while he (Crowle) went in search of her husband.

Hardneck was not a thoughtless man. Crowle hoped nothing bad had happened to the good-natured bull.

Despite the lateness of the hour there still seemed to be a lot of activity in the town. People were moving about in Main Street and the biggest saloon, the Bide In still seemed to be doing good business. Crowle went through the batwings. Everybody seemed to be talking at once and there was an air of excitement about the place. People moved aside for him without even seeming to notice him and, in a small town like this, that was unusual.

He breasted to the bar and the fat keep approached him. "Your pleasure, suh?"

"Rye."

He had a good drink before he asked his question, but then he did not whisper.

"I'm looking for Hardneck Gordino."

The effect was as if he had drawn a gun and shot a hole in the ceiling. All conversation in the immediate vicinity ceased abruptly.

Then somebody said huskily, "Tell him, Whip."

The fat barman said: "Hardneck's in jail, mister."

They obviously expected the newcomer to ask questions. They obviously wanted to ask some themselves. But he did not give them a chance either way.

He emptied his glass. "Thanks," he said and he turned away from the bar and made his way out.

He heard somebody say, "Did you see that badge?"

He did not think he knew the sheriff in this town, unless it was somebody from way back. Elderly lawmen often finished up in towns like this one.

The man was indeed elderly—somewhat older than Crowle anyway. He was a long man with grey side-burns and a worried look. His name was Ep Leary and Crowle did not know him. Leary had heard of Marshal Crowle, however, and was more than willing to explain to the marshal why Hardneck Gordino now languished in one of the two cells in back of the office.

Lazy Bend had a good jail, and its worried-looking custodian seemed a conscientious sort of gent. "You can tell me all of it before I look in on Hardneck," said the famous marshal. And he couldn't be fairer than that.

"It was the two men who had a run-in with Hardneck this afternoon. After they insulted Mrs Gordino."

"I heard about that," said Crowle.

"They're both dead. Shot in the back. And Hardneck was there at the time."

"What do you mean—he was there at the time?"

The sheriff looked uncomfortable. "Hardneck is

what you might call a friend o' mine. He's a very likeable sort of gent."

"Yeh," said the other man, not giving a fraction.

The sheriff went on: "Hardneck says he was going up the alley. That's the alley leading to the drinking place called The Mexican's. The door to the place is in the alley, an' that door is always ajar. Hardneck says he saw the two men come through the door and turn and walk towards him but he didn't recognise them because what light there was was behind them. He says he saw this other fellow come out of the door behind them and shoot them in the back, firing four shots, two for each of them.

"Then the fellow turned and ran down the alley in the other direction, Hardneck says. He chased the fellow. He shot at the fellow, more than once, but did not think he hit him. He says the fellow must have had a horse waiting out there and he galloped away.

"Other folks were brought out by the shooting of course. But nobody heard the sound of galloping hooves. I checked Hardneck's gun. Four shots had been fired."

"So you put him in jail," said Crowle.

Ep Leary did not directly answer this purely rhetorical question, which was maybe more of a statement after all. He said:

"This is a funny town. Although it is still only a small town, it is a very old one and there's a good proportion of the original settlers still here. To them, Hardneck Gordino is a Johnny-come-lately. To some of 'em even

I am a Johnny-come-lately. Hardneck is a respectable married ranch-man now. But to many of the goodfolk hereabouts he is still a rough ex-prizefighter with more than a flavour of the owlhoot trails about him too. They are quite willing to believe that those two dead hardhats were old saddle-pards of Hardneck's and the killings were due to some old grudge . . ."

The sheriff paused. Crowle did not say anything. The sheriff ploughed on doggedly. "It all looked mighty suspicious anyway. I put Hardneck in jail."

Crowle said: "Folks saw the two men in the place called The Mexican's, I guess?"

"Oh, yes."

"How about the other man then, the man that Hardneck says he saw?"

"Everybody says the two men were on their own all night."

"Did they see anybody follow them out?"

"No-o-o. You know what those places are like, everybody busy drinking."

"I haven't seen that place. But can I talk to Hardneck now?"

"Surely, marshal." Ep Leary got the keys, led the way.

Hardneck was surprised to see Crowle, but delighted also. The story he told his old friend had not altered one jot from the one he had told the sheriff earlier, and the worried-looking lawman was the first to admit this.

"Had you ever seen those two characters before?"

"No, Amos."

Crowle turned to the sheriff. "Can I take a look at the carcases?"

"Surely. But I have to stay right here."

"Just point me in the right direction then."

"Surely."

FIVE

Nobody was going to bed very early that night, and the local undertaker was still up.

He was a bit disgruntled when this lean stranger with a badge on his breast and an authoritative manner demanded to see the corpses before he (his name was Gupel) had had a chance to make them look more presentable. But there was something in those slate-grey eyes that gave the man the feeling that he was safer with the dead.

"This way, suh," he said.

The lawman inspected the corpses but had no comment to make. He merely said 'Much obliged, suh' and left. He had not bothered to take his hat off.

He returned to the law office. He said to the sheriff, "I know those two. I *knew* them, that is."

"I don't have dodgers on 'em. I looked. I had 'em in jail earlier. After they insulted Mrs Gordino. But she wouldn't swear out a complaint. I let 'em go. Now I wish to hell I hadn't. Who were they?"

"Ryley Jimson and his friend, Bick Something—I

disremember his full name. No, maybe there ain't dodgers out on them. They weren't very big potatoes. But they used to run with the Lemmy Spring bunch."

"I heard of that bunch," said Ep Leary. "But I also heard Lemmy was dead and the bunch split to hell and gone."

"Yeh, I heard that too. I'm willing to believe that the bunch has split up. They made things pretty hot for themselves in different parts of the West. And that story seems to be borne out by the fact of Ryley and Bick being on the loose. But, somehow, I don't figure their old boss, Lemmy Spring, is actually dead."

"Did Hardneck ever ride with the Spring bunch, do you think?"

"I very much doubt it. Hardneck was never a gangster. Most of the time he rode with but one man, a cantankerous, miserable runt called Laughing Luke Benteen. After Luke was killed Hardneck linked up with old Brackburn who is working for him at the spread now."

"Yeh, I know that. Hardneck and the old man used to do the fight circuits together. I saw Hardneck fight a couple of times. That was certainly something."

"I think Hardneck's fighting days are well over. Unless he's pushed."

"I hope they're over," said the sheriff and he sounded as if he meant it.

"Let me talk to him again, will you?"

"Surely."

By first light the following day Amos Crowle was on the trail again.

And Hardneck Gordino was still in jail.

Crowle had not had much sleep. But he was a man who did not need much sleep.

He had left a ticklish situation back in Lazy Bend. Although he hated to admit it, he knew that for the time being Hardneck should stay in jail, that he was maybe safer in jail. He had tried to explain this to Oggie, and she had believed him because she knew his way of law. But he had seen the sorrow like a shadow deep in her blue eyes. He had asked old Brackburn to watch over Oggie. The old man did not have to be told. His manner towards Crowle was not nearly so affable as it had been. But Crowle knew that Brackburn would not do anything foolish, that 'the missus' would be his prime concern.

In the early light that morning Crowle had covered the ground behind The Mexican's and had found signs of where a horse had been ground-hitched to a small round border, had cropped sparse grass as he stood waiting. There were the marks of bootheels too, signs of one horse, one horse-man. And they had gone away, fast, in the direction that Hardneck had indicated.

Crowle had had more luck at The Mexican's than Sheriff Ep Leary. But maybe that was because he was a whole lot more forceful than the elderly lawman, and he had a reputation behind him too.

He had seen dens like that the length and the breadth of the great Southwest. He knew the kind of people who used them, and they knew him. They called him Black Heart.

They had been a pretty sorry bunch at The Mexican's. In a place like Lazy Bend, a little tight town, there were very little pickings for such as they. They used The Mexican's as a sort of way station. As long as they sang small while they were in town, Ep Leary let them be. Ep was no gun-slinger, but he was a pretty wise old bird, and a fair man too, with the standards of the older and the best lawmen—while many of the younger breed were politicking all over the place and selling highly-inflated stories of their own exploits to Eastern tabloids and pulp publishers.

Those two saddle-tramps, Ryley Jimson and Bick Whatever-his-name-was had used The Mexican's as a way station. Or maybe they had actually had a rendezvous there. They had ridden into town together, but they could have arranged to meet somebody else there. Whether or not, somebody had caught up with them, and had not stopped to talk.

In The Mexican's Crowle had met an oldster he knew vaguely from way back, and who had very little truck with anybody, a bottle being his constant companion. Crowle had not had time to ask the old man how he had finally finished up in Lazy Bend. He had heard from this character, as well as from others, that nobody else had been with Ryley and Bick.

Crowle's old acquaintance, who always sat alone and whose bleary eyes saw more than one would have expected, had told the ol' Black Heart a mite more. He had seen a feller go out of the door behind Ryley and Bick. He thought it was the feller who had been sitting near the door. He had not seen that feller afterwards.

What did that feller look like?

He had worn spectacles and had a brown derby pulled over his eyes. The old man hadn't seen a brown derby like that since he was in Houston years ago. Otherwise, he said, that feller had been dressed like any other working drover or fiddlefooting waddy.

"But," the old man said, "what I saw of his face looked kinda white, kinda strange." He could not put in any different to that. A medium-sized, medium-built, medium-aged feller in a brown derby hat and steel-rimmed ordinary sort of spectacles and a kind of strange white face. It was a description that did not fit anybody Crowle had ever known. It did not fit a photograph, sketch or description on a Wanted notice that Crowle had ever seen.

A professional? But where from?

And why would anybody want two small potatoes like Ryley and Bick dead?

Nobody else remembered the feller in the brown derby hat and spectacles. But, still and all, you got all kinds in The Mexican's. And all kinds of hats. All kinds of weird mixtures of apparel in fact, and spectacles too. One of the regulars wore a black eye-patch, another an ornate beaded headband that he had taken from an Indian squaw, after he had raped her and killer her, 'twas said. There was one man, an English gambler, who wore a monocle, and there were plenty of garish scarves and Stetsons and sombreros and different shapes of felt hats and round prairie bowlers, though these were a rusty black, not brown . . .

Crowle rode. And in jail Hardneck waited.

Crowle thought he was doing the right thing; *him*. He hoped to God he was!

But he could not be too long away. If he lost the trail he would have to turn back.

He kept thinking about the bespectacled man in the brown derby hat whose trail he followed. His description did not fit in any way the description of gangleader Lemmy Spring with whom Ryley and Bick had ridden for a while. Did the man in the brown derby have any connection with Lemmy? Was Lemmy still alive, not dead as rumour had it? There was a big price on Lemmy's head.

But Lemmy was—or had been—a big man with a broad beefy red face and eyes like a demented eagle. Nothing like a medium-sized gent in spectacles with a strange white face. You could change your looks. Crowle had heard of wanted men who had had their faces cut by doctors, a messy process no doubt, a *shuddering* thing. But you could not get any doctor who could make you shrink . . .

The killer whom Crowle was following had ridden hard and had not tried to cover his trail. Crowle began to push his mount. Things would be a whole lot simpler if he could catch up with his man out in the great lonesome.

He followed a narrow winding not-too-clear trail

through a small range of hills, little more than large bumps in the all-over flatness, just conglomerations of rocks and sandhills. A man could hide here though, and a horse. Crowle did not pause much, but he kept low in the saddle. A man had to take chances. To a man like Crowle taking chances was the breath of life. But only an idiot rode a hostile country as if he wore chain-mail and the gods were protecting him and him alone.

Crowle had had some near-escapes, some notable ones. He had been staked out in the sun for the buzzards to peck at. He had had both his hands shot up and one of them, his left one luckily, was still pretty useless and he wore a glove upon it.*

But he was still alive and he aimed to stay that way.

Nobody shot at him from cover yet this day and the sun was getting hotter and the air was like the breath of a fire-eating monster. When he got to the other side of the hills he halted his mount and raised himself in the saddle. He was glad to do this, for he had been getting backache.

He raised himself in the stirrups and shaded his eyes with his hand and tried to make something out of the brown blankness ahead of him. But he was staring into the sun and everything was a-shimmer and the sweat trickled down his back like warm oil.

He was still in New Mexico, this he knew. But he did not think he had seen this particular territory before.

*These episodes are described in 'Bells in an Empty Town' and 'The Hands of Amos Crowle'.

He wondered if his quarry had. He was perfectly certain now that there was a quarry. Hardneck was no back-shooter. Crowle did not think that the bearded giant was a liar either.

One thing Crowle did not know for sure, however, was that his quarry was still ahead of him. In the hills reading sign had become difficult, on the hard rock, in the shifting shale.

He took a pull at his canteen. He climbed down from the saddle and moved ahead a bit, leaving his mount cropping grass, sparse stuff yet, but a welcome sight to the beast after the barrenness they had just left and over which the sure-footed animal had daintily picked his way. He was a good horse. Brown and white, but no patchwork, not quite a 'paint'. He had a white patch over his left eye which gave him a clownish appearance.

His behaviour also was kind of clownish sometimes and he had nipped his rider a couple of times. Crowle had not had him all that long but a sort of guarded understanding had grown up between them.

When the man cussed, the horse snorted derisively. But he seemed to sense the time when, such as now, tomfoolery was not permissible.

"I think I've found something, boy," the man said. "I hope it's a right something."

The horse wandered over towards him. The man mounted up again.

SIX

Hardneck Gordino paced back and forth in his cell like a large, restless animal. A man of the plains, he hated being caged. It did bad things to him.

Oggie and Brackburn had been to see him. Oggie had told him to trust in Amos Crowle. But there had been pain deep in her blue eyes. Old Brackburn had been somewhat non-committal. Hardneck had heard his old friend badgering Sheriff Leary with questions afterwards but he had not been able to catch the words.

Hardneck was innocent. They all knew it. Even the sheriff seemed to know it. But he was playing things strictly by the book. And Hardneck, with the bitter frustration of a man caged for something he did not do, was more and more desirous of re-writing pages of that book. As the day went on, the cell became hotter, seemed to get smaller, as if the walls were moving in on him and he was to become entombed.

The town was noisy that day. There were shouting voices. The lanky Doctor Pierson visited the sheriff a couple of times and they confabbed, but Hardneck did not know about what. He couldn't help figuring it was about him. He began to get the idea that not everybody in town thought him innocent. He was not a townsman proper—and he was not their kind. Not everybody wanted his spread—small though it was—on their doorstep. And there were bigger people who would like to swallow him up . . .

I'm getting fanciful, thought Hardneck. He lay down on the narrow bunk in the cell and tried to rest. He must have dozed off.

He awakened suddenly, feeling that eyes were staring at him. The sun had moved away from the window and the cell was not so hot. Neither was it so light, however. Two men were looking through the bars.

Hardneck knew them by sight, had seen them around town. He did not know their names. Barflies, he thought. What did they want? Alarm flared in him as he rose from the bunk.

"Hallo, Hardneck," said one of them cheekily. The other one did not say a word.

They were of about Hardneck's own age. They acted tough. But they did not look much. Sheriff Ep Leary appeared behind. "These are my two deputies," he said.

Some deputies, thought Hardneck—but maybe they were all Leary had been able to get, and he must have figured he needed some.

Poor specimens! And an old sheriff who looked so worried he was like to burst with it.

Hardneck just glared at the three of them and lowered himself onto the bunk once more. Because it was so low he sat with his knees up, and spread apart. The three men went away. Hardneck's thoughts ate at him—a mixture of frustration and trepidation and rage. And the rage grew slowly, inexorably, became the main emotion. He was a good-natured slob, but he had never been a patient one.

It was noisy out in the streets again.

I ought to get out of here, he thought. But this small cell was a good strong one. And he had told Amos Crowle . . .

He was like a man in a box!

Tied up with black ribbon.

*   *   *

The sun was dying when Crowle saw the town.

As he got closer he saw that it had a dead, dilapidated look about it. Nothing moved there and no smoke rose. Despite the heat, though that was waning, people would need fires for cooking and now it was near to cooking-time.

It was not a large town. In fact, it was a small one, a settlement. It was similar to the one he had visited in the night before he had reached Lazy Bend, the one where that murdering rapist, Jacel, had met his final cumuppance. Jacel's summary execution at the hands of those small-ranchers had brought Crowle's job to an abrupt end. He could have turned back then; and, if it wasn't for the fact that he had friends in that territory, he would have done just that.

Now he was on the trail again. Jacel was under the sod, but nothing else seemed to have changed. Crowle had a sudden fatalistic idea that he was doomed to ride the trail forever in pursuit of the wrongdoers of this world. But he could not kill them all. He was no avenging angel. He was the devil that men called Black Heart . . .

Uncharacteristically, he had let his mind wander. And he almost paid dearly for that.

His hat was plucked from his head as if by the sweep of a fiery brand and, even as he was pitching from his horse he heard the familiar snap of a distant rifle—but not too distant. He grovelled on the ground, half-blinded by his own blood—he had never known his blood run so quickly! He thought the top of his head must have been taken off with the hat. He could not see the hat.

He could not see anything much, only that his horse had come to a halt and was between him and the distant buildings, was maybe sheltering him.

Crowle raised his hand to his head and winced. He had been neatly 'creased' across the crown. A couple of inches lower and the bullet would have taken his brains right along with his hat.

If the marksman had fired from the buildings he certainly was a shooting fool. But he should have waited just a mite longer!

Crowle was devoutly thankful that he hadn't.

He cursed himself. Lolly-gagging along, daydreaming like a gingham girl walking by the river with her first beau. Big tough gunslinger Amos Crowle, who had nearly got his goddam head blown off!

His horse stayed still. The rifleman did not fire again, obviously waiting for a better shot. He might even figure that he had got his man already.

Crowle took the bandanna from round his neck and tied it around his head, pulled it tight. With a raggedy handkerchief he took from his vest pocket he wiped the blood from his eyes and his brow. It still trickled, but it seemed to be running down his cheeks now and did not bother him so much. He felt, however, as if somebody had swiped him across the front of the cranium with a fence stake.

He spotted his hat and crawled to it. He managed to get it awkwardly on top of the bandage, holding the bandage in place. Already the blood was gumming there and the sore groove burned as if he had been branded with a running iron.

It's time I got off my knees, he thought. He reached the horse and grabbed the stirrup and hauled himself up, but not as high as the saddle, still covering himself. The horse turned his head and looked at him as if to say, what the hell are you playing at now, bucko?

Crowle reached up for the reins. "You move when I tell you, jackass," he said. "An' you move fast."

He hauled himself up into the saddle with a swiftness that caused the sky to swing over his head and the red ball of the lowering sun to plummet like a shattered pendulum. But already the horse was moving fast, and then the man crouched low, swung himself sideways like an Indian and, with a pressure of his knees, guided the horse at a tangent. They kept going in the same general direction but they veered away from the buildings.

The rifleman fired two shots but they went high. The horse was galloping full-out now and was a bad target, even for a sharpshooter as good as that one had seemed to be. But maybe his first shot had been a lucky one.

Soon Crowle knew they were out of range. And the rifleman knew it too. He did not essay a third shot, a fourth shot if you counted the first one, which could have put a stop to the whole match even before it started. I've got me a scar, thought Crowle, and I haven't fired a goddam single shot.

He guided the horse in a half-circle, not slowing him much, still trying to keep out of range. Then, when he figured he was almost directly on the other side of the buildings from where he had approached them in the first place, he changed the horse's direction again and sent him galloping forward at the buildings.

And Crowle was low in the saddle again.

He was out of the saddle and, half-crouching, sprinting for the nearest building when the rifleman opened up again. But he had reached his position too late. Crowle had momentarily outfoxed him. His first shot—obviously a hasty one—kicked up the dust at the heels of the running man.

The second bullet was closer but Crowle was protected from it, rolling through an open door and into a dusty interior, being showered with wood chips but nothing else.

He crouched by a shattered window. Most of the frame had gone as well as the glass. His gun was in his hand. He knew his horse was beside the building, in shelter, and within reach. His head thumped as if an invisible enemy was beating on it with a large mallet. But that one was not as lethal as the other invisible one outside and would doubtless go away eventually.

He had left his hat behind him somewhere. He turned his head. The battered Stetson lay in the doorway through which he had come. He left it where it was for the time being. His rush had carried him right across the room and now he could look out on an empty street.

This was a ghost town in which he found himself.

And now, in the silence, he could hear the sounds of creaking doors and banging shutters and the faint soughing of the breeze that had come up as the sun went down.

It was as if there had been a mass exodus from this town, almost a panic. As if everybody had decamped in a tearing hurry, leaving all doors and windows open behind them. There were a few items of furniture in the room where Amos Crowle crouched but none of it had gotten in his way as he propelled himself across the bare boards of the floor.

Opposite his position was a hotel. A leaning sign proclaimed that this was called 'The Splendide', a glaring exaggeration, a pocked sign, and a false front that leaned forth at a perilous angle. The street was littered with debris, for not all things had survived the winds.

There was nothing for Crowle out there, over there. He figured that his friend, the marksman, was somewhere on the same side of the street as himself. The direction from which those two rifle-shots had come had seemed to indicate this. Unless the man could move so fast that he had been able to whip across the street before Crowle was able to spot him. Unless there was more than one man, another one hidden someplace else, waiting.

Crowle waited now, got himself orientated, waited for his head to settle down a bit. He fingered the bandage there, pulled it back into place. Blood was crusted along his forehead, but the shallow wound had not opened again. His vision was clear. The thumping in his head began to abate. It settled down to a dull ache.

"Hey, mister!"

The shouting voice jolted him. It came from behind and over to the left he thought. It was high, rasping, querulous.

"What do you want?"

"Do you wear spectacles?" A surprising question.

"Hell, no. Never worn spectacles in my life."

"Where's your brown derby?" That question gave Crowle another jolt.

"Never worn a brown derby in my life either. You've got the wrong pigeon, *amigo*."

The voice gave a cackle. An old man's cackle. "I seed your hat when it bounced."

"It was almost my head that bounced. You loco or somep'n, oldtimer?"

"Nope. I just want to live to be a hundred that's all. But I'll take a chance on you."

"That's white of you. So what do we do next?"

"I'm going to put down my rifle and my gun and I'm coming out into the street. I'd like you to do the same."

"All right." Here goes another jackass, thought Crowle.

He took off his gunbelt and laid it gently on the bare dusty boards. The door was ajar. It squealed in protest when Crowle pushed it open wider. He moved onto the sagging, splintered broadwalk and looked towards the left. He saw the old man right away. He seemed to be unarmed. He did not have a rifle anyway.

They both stepped off the sidewalk. The street, despite its littered surface, was far less perilous. As they drew closer together they sized each other up. Crowle had a sneak derringer in his boot. The oldster was not wearing a gunbelt, but maybe he had a sneak weapon too. He looked like a canny old bird. Like a not too-well-fed eagle. With a big beaked nose in a narrow, wrinkled face and snappping eyes which seemed mischievous rather than wicked. With a lean frame and a loping bowlegged walk.

The old man had an extremely battered felt hat tilted to the back of his head, releasing wisps of grey hair. There was a nasty swelling blue-red bruise on his temple. His clothing was nondescript, his half-boots scuffed, concertina-ing, down-at-heel.

"You're not the feller," the old man said.

"You're damn right I'm not the feller," Crowle said.

"I hit you," the old man said. "I'm purely sorry, mister, I really am."

I could be stinking out there in the grass with a hole in my head, Crowle thought, and I ought to pop this old goat and leave him lie. But he had a sneaking admiration for the oldster's courage in taking a chance and coming out facing him like this. He had apologised most handsomely.

Hell, thought Crowle, all I have is a headache. He said:

"You look as if your head has come in contact with somep'n hard too."

"That's how come I was shooting at you," the oldster said. "I'll tell you about it. But let's get off the street first an' I'll fix that head for you."

"That's the least you can do," said Crowle sardonically.

The old man cackled and slapped his knee. "You're a humorous-type gent, ain't you?"

"Sometimes. An' I reckon that's lucky for you mebbe. Can you trust me to go back an' get my gun-rig and my hat?"

"I reckon so, young feller." He drew back into a nearby doorway. Crowle turned about. When he got back he had his hat on, awkwardly atop of the scarf, and he was buckling on his gunbelt. His movements made his vest swing back, revealing his badge.

"Godamighty," said the old man. "I shot me a lawman." For the first time, he looked a little apprehensive.

"I'll waive judgment," said Crowle. "Lead on, oldtimer."

"This way, suh . . . Name's Jake Boots."

"My name is Crowle. Amos Crowle."

"I heard o' you," the old man said.

SEVEN

Brackburn had been at loggerheads with the law for most of his adult life. He did not trust the law. And he did not trust lawmen. How his friend Hardneck, who was like a big son to him, could also make a friend of a lawman like Amos Crowle, Brackburn could not understand. Hardneck, like Brackburn, was an ex-owlhooter. Oh, sure, he was going straight now, and so was Brackburn. But, hell, that didn't mean to say they had to make goddam *friends* with the other side. And Crowle, with his reputation for dispensing a particularly ruthless type of justice, was definitely on the other side. So Brackburn listened to Hardneck, and he listened to Miz Oggie, but he kept his own counsel. He did not trust the law in any shape or form.

Now Hardneck was in jail for something he hadn't done. That was your 'respectable' law for you!

And Brackburn had more than a sneaking idea that the respectable upholders of law and order in Lazy Bend were all set to believe that the wild blackbearded man from the small ranch was a backshooting murderer. After all, he was not really 'their sort'.

They'll railroad him, thought Brackburn, they'll railroad the big good-natured bastard.

Like hell they will, he thought, I could break my hardnecked friend out of that tin-can jail without any trouble at all. With almost no trouble anyway.

Amos Crowle was not in town now. Amos Crowle had ridden away—supposedly in pursuit of the man who had actually murdered those two saddle-tramps. Amos Crowle might be away weeks. Amos Crowle might not come back at all!

Brackburn went to the house and talked to Oggie.

At first she did not see eye-to-eye with him. But Brackburn was a very persuasive old man. He could see that the woman was worried sick about her husband and, stifling his great affection for her, he played upon her uncertainties and her fears. It is all a means to an end, he thought.

She said: "Amos will come back."

"Maybe he will. But it might take longer than we think. And imagine what the wait will do to Hardneck. Besides, I don't trust those townspeople . . ."

"They wouldn't . . ."

"Don't bet on no wouldn'ts, missus. I've seen towns like this one before, and I've been in their jails."

"Sheriff Leary is a good man."

"Granted. But weak. And he's only one man. And he put Hardneck in there. He didn't have to. Hardneck is innocent."

"I know."

"So I've got to get him out."

"You can't. You . . ."

"I can. Trust in me."

"I do. But . . ."

"But me no buts." He was talking to her like a father now. "Get the waggon ready with all the stuff you need."

"We'll have to leave the ranch . . ."

"What good is the ranch with Hardneck in jail—or worse?"

It was that 'or worse' that did it.

"All right," she said. "I will do what you say. And I will wait." There was a weariness in her voice.

"Trust in me," said Brackburn, for the second time.

* * *

The two townsfolk—if they could be termed that— hired as deputies by Sheriff Leary were called Jigger and O'Sanderson. They had done many things in their comparatively short lives, but they had never been deputies before. They preened themselves—and when the sheriff left them in charge of the jail while he went to get some belated chow they assured him that they would guard it with their lives, or words to that effect.

They had come from another part of the country and had been friends since they were boys at school together. They had not put in much time at school anyway and had run away as soon as they were tall enough and able. They were not bad men, not even regular hardcases, just a little much addicted to booze and to getting money without actually working for it.

They did not have much respect for the law or for the people who administered it—a bigger lot of double-dealers, Jigger and O'Sanderson thought, than the folks on the other side of the fence, and that fence at times was a mighty shaky thing. The best thing about Jigger and O'Sanderson was their friendship, their loyalty to each other.

They had their feet on the sheriff's big desk and were sprawled in a chair apiece when somebody knocked on the door. It was not three spaced knocks, the way the sheriff had said he would signal to them.

O'Sanderson was nearest to the door and he let the front legs of his chair hit the boards with a thump. He slid from it and stood upright.

"Watch yourself," said Jigger. He rose too, as O'Sanderson made for the door. O'Sanderson drew his gun. Jigger followed suit, moved over a bit, watched his partner.

The door was bolted. O'Sanderson put his face close to it and called, "Who is that?"

A gruff voice replied, "The sheriff sent some eats over for you boys."

Old Brackburn had watched the sheriff leave the office and go into a nearby hashhouse. He had waited till Leary was settled at his late supper and then, shotgun swinging negligently in his hand, he had crossed the street.

He already had two horses waiting in an alley, the other side of the jail from the hashhouse, which was a lucky thing.

It was a simple ploy. And the simplicity of it worked like a black cat charm.

"That was mighty nice of the sheriff," said O'Sanderson. He glanced over his shoulder. "Supper!"

"Fine," said Jigger. "I am kinda peckish."

O'Sanderson shot the bolt, turned the key, opened the door. In order to do this he transferred his gun to his left hand, held it dangling there.

When Brackburn came quietly into Lazy Bend he had had no settled plan in mind and, after stashing the two horses, he had watched the office for a few minutes before he saw the sheriff come out. But now luck was with the old jail-breaker right down the line.

The door opened and the man had a gun but it was not lifted.

Brackburn rammed the barrel of his shotgun into the man's belly and said: "Drop it, bucko, an' back up."

O'Sanderson dropped the gun and made a few halting steps backwards, shooting a glance over his shoulder at his pard.

"Drop your iron, Jigger," said Brackburn. "Or this one gets a hole in him." He knew these boys' names anyway. He saw Jigger drop the gun. "Join him, O'Sanderson," he said.

He made the two men, with Jigger toting the keys, lead him into the cell-block.

Hardneck had heard the voices, had recognised that of his cantankerous authority-hating old friend, so he had half-known what to expect. He did not object to being let out of jail. He fetched a lariat from out of the office and helped Brackburn to tie up the two deputies, gagging them with their own scarves.

The old man had brought a gun for his big friend, but neither of them needed a weapon now. They got out of town without seeing another soul.

And, back at the little ranch Oggie was waiting.

*　　*　　*

It was night.

Jake Boots said: "When I came round he had gone and he had taken most of my grub and my coffee and my whisky an' my hoss. He left his own hoss behind. The pore beast's lame, but I ain't had the heart to do anything about him yet." He tied a final knot, patted the bandage on Crowle's head with gnarled fingers. "How's that feel?"

"All right."

Boots went on: "He should have killed me instead of just laying me out. I guess he didn't realise I had recognised him. He certainly didn't recognise me."

"Who is he?"

"He's called Max Railham and he's a professional killer."

"If he had killed you he wouldn't have got paid for it," said Amos Crowle.

"I hadn't thought o' that."

"Where did you meet him?"

"I ain't incriminating myself."

"You won't. I'm no lawyer. I'm just a lawman doing

a job, one job at a time."

"I used to cook for the Lemmy Spring gang."

"Do tell! I heard Lemmy was dead."

"Yeh, I heard that too. Do you know how he died?"

"Nope. Do you believe he is dead?"

"If he ain't," said Boots, "he ought to be lying low. I guess he's wanted in about every state in the West, ain't he? You'd know more about that than I do, you bein' a lawman an' all."

"He's wanted pretty badly all right . . . But, go on, you tell me your story."

"I live here alone," said Boots. "I ain't exactly a gabby ol' goat but I do get purty tired o' talking to animals. It's mighty nice to talk to people once in a while. Max Railham didn't give me much time."

"How much?"

"None. He held me up. Then he hit me." The old man leaned forward. "But do you know somep'n, marshal, I think he's still around this area someplace."

EIGHT

Ep Leary took his time over his late supper. He had been hellishly hungry and now he was eating a lot, savouring it. Hot pie and greens and roast potatoes, with thick gravy in a large carafe at his side. He had made good use of this. The town was fairly quiet now. The good folk had already gone to bed, and maybe most of the not-so-good had done the same, with a bottle, with a woman, maybe with nothing at all, though they would wake with a fatter head in the morning.

Earlier it had seemed as if trouble threatened. There had been a lot of loud talk. Sometimes, as Sheriff Ep knew, this could lead to hellish things. But in this case it had not done so. Maybe that was because Ep had gotten himself a couple of volunteer deputies, such as they were. They would stand guard though, and he did not think anybody was going to bother them.

The speciality of the hashhouse in which Ep now sat was pies, all kinds of pies. Now, to bank up his meal the sheriff had a huge hunk of apricot and apple pie with thick custard and then coffee and a cheroot and he leaned back in his chair and smoked expansively.

He felt he had done the right thing all along and that things were going to work out fine.

There were only two other people in the dining-place. A gambler and a girl. They rose now and the gambler called "Goodnight, sheriff."

"Goodnight."

The man was inoffensive. All he loved was cards and women and he was reputed to be pretty straight as card-sharps go. You've got to live and let live, Ep thought, and a man in his position could not afford to be too much of a blue-nose. This was a pretty tidy billet he had now, and he sure as hell wasn't getting any younger.

The proprietress, Widow Shane, came in and asked him if he wanted anything else.

"No, thanks, Mamie," he said. "That was fine, I'll tell you. Mighty fine."

"Do you want to come in back for a drink, Ep?"

He hesitated before replying. A drink in the back late at night always led to other things, maybe a whole night of other things and him creeping back to his billet at dawn. There had been a thing between him and Mamie, ever since just after her husband died of a rotting liver. But they had both kept their own independence and the 'night occasions' had been less frequent of late. Again Ep was reminded that he sure as hell wasn't getting any younger; he was no chick. He remembered he had his duty and a prisoner in the jailhouse and two deputies who were certainly not the

best two deputies he could have got. He had to get back!
He told Mamie so and she agreed, pouting
characteristically with full red lips, but not looking too
disappointed. Her fine dark eyes looked tired and there
were crows' feet at the corners. She was an Autumn hen
now all right.

He watched her go away. She had fine womanly hips
and her waist had not thickened too much with the
years. But there was a rounded, tired droop to her
shoulders. Ep began to feel kind of guilty, but he was
not sure what he was feeling guilty about. He finished
his cheroot and rose and put on his hat.

"Goodnight, honey," he called.

From the back she answered him throatily. He
remembered how that husky voice used to stir him not
so long ago. Or maybe it was longer ago than he
thought. And time kept movin' on, as the man said. It
had moved on tonight. Hell, yes, he had to get back.

There was nobody near his office. He gave the three
spaced knocks that were the pre-arranged signal, so
that one of the boys could shoot the bolt and unlock the
door and let him in.

He waited. He listened. There was no sound of
movements from inside. He looked about him. Nothing
moved, neither animal or human. He knocked again.
There was still no reply and he put his face to the door
and called guardedly, "Jigger—O'Sanderson."

There was no answering voice and nothing else
happened. Ep tried the door. He could not budge it.
What were those two jackasses playing at?

He left the front door and went round the back. The back door was closed but he discovered to his surprise that it was not locked. Now he became suspicious. He drew his gun before cautiously pushing the door open. Nothing happened. But then he heard the noises. Scufflings. And what sounded like pigs grunting. Coming from the direction of the cell-block.

His two brand-new deputies were trusted up like turkeys ready for the pot, in the cell once occupied by Hardneck Gordino. There was no sign of Hardneck. The cell-door was locked and there was no sign of the keys. He could not ask the boys where the keys were as they were both gagged, their eyes looking at him imploringly from over the top of what appeared to be their own kerchiefs. They made inarticulately obscene noises and squirmed as if their water was already coming to the boil.

Maybe they did not know where the keys were. Maybe the folk who had overpowered them and set Hardneck loose had taken the keys with them. And Ep only had the one bunch. He had had a second one but had lost it a couple of months ago. He had been meaning to get copies . . .

He had been meaning to do lots of things.

He searched the outside passages, the second cell, the office, his quarters, hoping that maybe he would even find that second bunch. But he found no keys at all.

* * *

Crowle did not have to believe all of Jake Boots' story.

Nobody told a story straight, particularly a story like that one.

Boots had been a trail cook and a good one, he said. But at that particular time, the time he was talking about, he had not had a job and had been pretty much on his uppers. This had been in a little town down on the Pecos—he disremembered its name.

Then this feller had approached him. A big handsome feller with a big beefy face and hot, wicked eyes. He had said that his bunch needed a cook and a man who knew how to handle a gun. Boots was no gunslinger, only a middling gunhand. He had seen plenty worse though. And, for the other thing, if the feller could find a better eats-handler in this territory he—Jake Boots—would eat his own hat. That was what he told the feller.

The feller laughed kind of nastily and said he hoped Boots had a nice way of cooking hats, with sauce an' all. But he also said he would take a chance on Boots.

Judging this feller for the kind of extreme hard-nut that he was, Boots figured that he had better come through with some prime cooking or he might be forced to eat his own headgear, with or without sauce.

He had been uneasy. But he had been very hungry too.

The feller said his name was Spring, and the name did not register on Boots right then. Spring did not tell Boots anymore and Boots didn't think it would be good politics to question the big dangerous-looking coot. He went along.

That was during the time that Lemmy Spring and his then-bunch spent many of their night hours in the stealing of other folks' beef and were not averse to shooting up a few ranches and their drovers at the same time.

"I didn't go along on those raids, Mistuh Crowle. It was my job to see to the hot coffee and the eats when they got back and maybe do a few jobs o' patching if the going had been rough. I helped to bury more than one owlhooter in some lonely spot and I was the only one who said the words over 'em."

"Go on." It was a non-committal remark, no comment, not even an encouragement. This lean, dark man with a badge on his vest, a black moustache, slate-grey eyes, and a left hand which he never seemed to take out of his glove, was as hard as Lemmy Spring had been, if in a subtly different way. Jake Boots went on:

"Lemmy paid me well, I'll say that for him. And he didn't ask me to do any shooting—I'll swear to that." The old man gave his cackling laugh. "Mebbe he was scared o' me getting perforated permanent and he would lose a mighty fine cook . . . I'd do you something now, suh, but Max Railham took it all."

"You were going to tell me about Max Railham. Was he with the bunch when you first joined 'em?"

"No. He came later." Boots paused. Then he went on in a rush. "Lemmy had turned from cattle to banks. He said you could do 'em in the daytime and have your drinks and your woman at night like a natural man should, though, hell, he was no natural man. He was all killer. Maybe he chose banks because he might kill more people that way. Anyway, he said they were easy. And, of course, there wasn't all the trouble of driving stolen cattle to a buyer, of using a running iron on the brands and all that sort of thing.

"We were not on the trail so much. The bunch didn't need me so much. I thought of pulling out, but I figured that Lemmy mightn't take kindly to me doing it without warning. He had made people dead for less than that. He was a great one for loyalty, which meant you did what he said or you suffered the consequences. I bided my time. I waited for an opportunity . . ."

And during that time you maybe helped to stick up a few banks, thought Crowle sardonically. But he did not say anything. And, after a short pause, Jake Boots went on with his tale.

"I didn't get an opportunity. Not yet, not then. Lemmy wanted to take a big bank, but he didn't want to do it in the old in-an'-out shoot-up way. He liked shooting folks, but he didn't like his own folks getting shot up too.

"He picked a bank in San Antonio. But it had two bank guards, two brothers called Regoni who were supposed to be hell in boots, had notches on their guns from the outlaws they had killed. Lemmy sent for Max Railham, hired him to assassinate the two men in his own particular way . . . Railham isn't a Westerner you know. He comes from someplace in the East, I dunno where. He doesn't talk like us." Boots was slowing down again. His eyes were squinted almost shut in his wrinkled face, as if he was trying to remember things.

He continued at a slower, more halting pace. "Railham found out that the brothers lived in a frame house on the outskirts of San Antone, that they lived alone except for an old Mexican woman who kept house for them, and she went home to her family of nights. They were well-known womanisers and had girls there from time to time, but it didn't seem like there were any permanents.

"They always walked to work the same way, through their own back garden, sort of making a detour round the backs of town, their women with them on some mornings. They were discreet and they were deadly. But they tended their garden which was the best for miles.

"Railham waited for them in that garden, which had much shrubbery. He shot them in the back and a girl who happened to be with them. One brother had gone to bed with a bottle that night instead of with a woman. All three died instantly and nobody even heard the shots, which were blanketed by the house and the garden, it bein' out back an' on the edge of town.

"Lemmy and the boys hit the bank and came away with quite a haul. Nobody got hurt that time. Nobody in the bank, no passerby, none of Lemmy's boys. So, it seemed, Railham had come in pretty handy, getting rid of the Regoni brothers like he did early on that very morning. He didn't stay with the gang though, Railham. He had done the job he was hired for and he had been paid. He moved on. He's a loner. A real professional . . ."

"A backshooter too," put in Crowle, remembering how back in Lazy Bend, Ryley and Bick had got it in the back, just the way the Regoni brothers had all those years ago. How many jobs had Max Railham had between those times and how many of them had come easy, backshot bullets and a retreat in the night?

"Just after that," Boots said, "Lemmy got a bullet in his leg and was laid up and I took my opportunity and lit out. We were back in the Pecos country. Lemmy seemed to like it down there. I crossed Texas an' came to New Mexico. I worked on chuck waggons. I got kinda old. Then one day I found this place an' I've been here ever since." He leaned back. He had run his string.

"You tell a good story, old man."

"It's the gospel truth, Mistuh Crowle."

NINE

Sheriff Ep Leary had awakened the local locksmith to help him get the cell-door open. While the two cursing men worked, the trussed deputies watched them with wild eyes and tried, not too-successfully, to add their own expletives to the general run of ultimately basic rhetoric. O'Sanderson's red hair stood on end like the comb of a fighting cock. His partner, Jigger, had long greasy black locks and they kept getting in his eyes.

The locksmith was not a very good locksmith. He broke a few of his implements and bent a few more and he did not get the door open. So Ep decided to do what maybe he should have done in the first place. He told himself that he had not done this because he might endanger his two deputies who, trussed as they were, could not possibly move. But he finally fired four shots from his Colt and the lock was blown apart and amid a haze of blue smoke the door swung open.

A piece of flying metal had grazed O'Sanderson's upper left arm, cutting through his shirt and bringing blood. But, unless he got blood-poisoning, he wasn't about to be slowed down at all. Jigger was unhurt, but he had cursed so much through his gag that he had almost ruined his voice, could only talk in a hoarse croak.

Neither men had contemplated going on a manhunt. So soon too. They had only been lawmen a matter of hours. But they were both so enraged by the way they had been tricked—and trussed—that their stronger feelings overcame their usually highly-developed instinct for self-preservation and they let the sheriff lead them.

It was early morning and too much time had been lost already. Ep's shooting-off his gun so early had brought to light a good measure of irate populace, but nobody offered to join a posse.

"To hell with them," said Ep petulantly.

On his way out of town with O'Sanderson and Jigger he saw the early-awake Widow Shane and she waved to him gaily as if she thought he was going fishing or something. He now devoutly wished he had taken her up last night and stayed for coffee and whatever followed it . . . His two inept new-fish deputies would still have been trussed—and serve 'em goddam right!

Already, now they were on the trail, he had grave doubts about Jigger and O'Sanderson. How would they stack up against two curly wolves like Hardneck and Brackburn, two curly wolves who had reverted to type? And there was Oggie Gordino, a very forthright woman, who made the odds even. Maybe I should have waited, thought Ep. But for how long? Until he got a posse? *If* he got a posse. Maybe the only volunteer would have been old Doc Pierson, who was game for pretty much anything but was certainly no gunfighter.

One minute I don't want to do anything much, thought Ep, not even spend a night with Mamie Shane, the next I'm going off half-cocked like a young sprig with his pecker on fire.

So much had happened lately. All at once it seemed. So a body went along and just did what a body thought it ought to do. And this particular body, somewhat decrepit though it had lately become, was the elected representative of the law in this here territory.

Hell, I'm committed, thought Ep, and he suddenly felt almost lighthearted about it.

The three men reached the little Gordino spread. The place was empty. They found the waggon-tracks. The vehicle had obviously been loaded. There were signs of horses too, but they could not tell how many. The corral was empty.

"They've had a hell of a start I reckon," Ep said, "but the waggon's bound to slow 'em down. Come on, boys, let's get on the trail."

He aimed to follow that bunch to the end of his area of jurisdiction. What he aimed to do if he caught up with them he had not figured yet.

'The boys' followed him. They had been pretty vociferous since they left town. Jigger had got most of his voice back. The cussing part of it anyway. But now both of them were silent and Ep felt as if he were pulling them along on the end of a long lariat, as if he were the goat leading them to the slaughter.

* * *

Crowle awoke in the morning with a splitting headache and at first did not know where he was, which was unusual for him. He soon came to full awareness though. The band of fire across his head reminded him of what had happened. At the same time the smell of frying bacon assailed his nostrils.

Old Jake Boots came into view. "It's quiet out there," he said.

Crowle said: "I thought Max Railham took all your supplies."

"I've got a small cache hidden in a cellar. Leastways I did have. I'd figured it was empty an' needed replenishing an' Railham wouldn't have got anything even if he found the place. But I took me a look this morning and found a small roll o' bacon in a corner. I ain't got no coffee or anything like that but there's still some whisky left."

Crowle remembered the whisky from last night. They had drunk some of it with some salt pork and a can of beans that Crowle had had along with him.

"An' I've still got a tank full of water," cackled Boots.

The bottle of whisky had been suspended in the water and it was something else Railham had missed, though he hadn't missed much it seemed.

"That jasper has been in the West for years," Boots said. "But in some ways he's still just a tenderfoot. I think he's scared of being left in the open lands without chow, that's why he took all mine. With the heat comin' on like it is, a lot of it's gonna go bad before he can get around to eating it. I hope it gives him the raving cobble-wobbles."

"I thought you figured he might be still around here someplace," said Crowle, digging into the greasy bacon on the tin plate.

Boots placed beside the lawman a shot-glass of whisky with a modicum of water. It was soft water from a spring about three miles from the ghost town and it went well with the whisky, which wasn't particularly high-class, just kind of biting when taken neat.

Boots said now, "An old man's fancies I guess. Why would he hang around in this area after he had got what he wanted?"

"No reason. Unless he saw me ride in and figures me for the opposition and is waiting for a chance to pot me."

They had stood watch, turn and turn about. Cat-napping anyway. Neither of them had seen or heard anything. I should be getting after that killer, Crowle thought. His headache was getting better.

He had asked Boots how he managed to live in this place. He had learned that the old man had panned in the spring where he got his water and had come up with some dust. This was after his available money had gone and he had been thinking of leaving the place he called 'his town' and hitting the chuck-waggon trail again. Or maybe, in his old age, getting a job in some hashhouse. But it seemed he was fated to stay here. And he was

happy to do this, until he got completely old and slow—
or even sick—and craved human company again.

He was no lover of people, he said, he had seen too
many of 'em. But everybody needed a friend sometimes. The old man seemed to have accepted Crowle
completely, after getting close to killing him. But now
he was quite open and trusting with the famous lawman.

Reverting to the subject of his dust again now that
the morning was here, Boots said: "Do you think that
that Railham jasper might have got some idea there
might be gold pickings around here?"

"I doubt it," said Crowle. "He's on the run. He killed
two men back in a town called Lazy Bend. That's why
I'm after him. A friend of mine is in jail on suspicion of
the crime. Railham shot the two men in the back."

"It figures!"

"Those two men. Their names were Ryley Jimson
and Bick Something-or-other . . ."

"Bick Manders," said Boots quickly. "Ryley Jimson
and Bick Manders. They ran with Lemmy Spring."

"Were they on the San Antonio bank job, the one
that featured Max Railham in his well-known position
as back-shooter?"

Jake Boots' already much-wrinkled brow became as
corrugated as an iron-sheet roof. Then his eyes widened
and he slapped his knee.

"No," he said. "They weren't on that job. I'm sure of
it. Lemmy picked his men for that. I'm pretty sure he
wouldn't have used Ryley and Bick, even if they were

around at the time. He only used 'em as waddies when he was on a rowdy sort of job like running-off cattle or treeing a town an' milking it."

"So it's very probable that Ryley and Bick didn't know Railham?"

"Sure. Very probable."

Crowle changed his tack. "What was that little town you mentioned to me?"

Boots had earlier mentioned a town where he got his supplies.

"It's called Balkan an' it's about seven miles from here."

"Funny name for a town."

"Yeh. Lots o' foreigners there. Religious sects an' sechlike. None of 'em ever come here. They think the place is haunted by dead Injuns or somep'n. Do you know what this ghost town was called before it became a ghost town?"

"Nope."

Boots cackled. "No Hope. No Hope, that was what it was called. There was gold around here y'see. But then it petered out and the grass ain't all that good and the soil ain't all that good an' people just moved. That was before I came. There was plenty of hope I guess but that went too. Maybe some man with comical ideas named the place No Hope—or maybe it was because, before the gold strike, it was the site of an Injun massacre, or supposed to be."

Crowle said: "There are so many places in the West now that are supposed to have been sites of Injun massacres that it's sometimes a wonder to me that there are any of us whites left."

Boots cackled. "You're right there, pardner."

"Hell, folks are so goddam superstitious. Some o' the whites are worse than the Injuns. Scared o' boogie-men . . . Anyway, you found gold here afterwards, didn't you, this place has been good to you?"

"Dust," said Boots scornfully. "Yaller dust. Hardly enough to keep body an' soul together an' keep 'em functioning."

"Just as you say, oldtimer," said Crowle, wondering if Jake Boots was keeping something from him. He rose. "I'm gonna ride on to that town. I figure it would be Max Railham's next port, particularly if he is as scared of starving as you think he is. He'll be after more supplies, won't he?"

"Yeh, unless he's aiming to by-pass the town, using my stuff."

"And then what would be his next port?"

"Hell only knows! A long way on I guess."

"So." Crowle began to walk.

"Do you mind if I mosey along with you? I gotta get me some more supplies, don't I?"

"I guess. Let's travel then."

TEN

Hardneck said: "Tall Lincrane might not even be there. He might be off on the circuits. But I'm known there so it should be all right, unless it's full of new boys I don't know from Hades. Lot o' newcomers in the fight game now, some of 'em even using gloves, so I've heard."

"You never used gloves, did you, pard?" said old Brackburn. "Neither did Tall."

"Nope. 'Cept in training o' course, with sparring partners. Didn't do to mark up good sparring partners too much. An' a man could break his hand."

"Not your hand, pard."

"No. But I wasn't in the game all that long, was I? Not nearly as long as Tall. And, as far as we know, he's still in it. And I never heard of Tall breaking a hand."

"Me neither," said Brackburn.

Oggie had been looking from one to the other of the two men with a hint of exasperation in her bright blue eyes. Hardneck turned to her and said: "You remember Tall don't you, honey? Last time we seen him he was working for Amos Crowle, deputying, and they called at the spread one night."*

"Of course I remember Tall," said Oggie tartly.

"As I remember too, you doctored Amos's bad hand," Hardneck said.

"Yes."

"You was away then, oldtimer."

"Yes," said Brackburn. "I remember you told me about it afterwards. You didn't know Crowle all that well then though, did you?"

"Nope. Not at all. He ain't gonna like what we're doing now."

"It's too damn' late for us to do anything about that now," snorted Brackburn. "Beggin' your pardon, Miz Oggie."

"Granted."

"I see Crowle still wears a glove on that left hand," said Brackburn. "Maybe he ain't quite so smart and armour-plated as you think."

"Like you said, oldtimer, it's too late to do anything about that now."

"Durn' tootin!" said Brackburn.

Hardneck put the conversation back on its original tack, saying, "There ain't many people 'cept those in the fight game knows about this place." He gestured ahead. "The boys don't like anybody to know about their form. It interferes with the betting. I remember a fancy-talkin' gambler found his way there oncet. He

*See 'Black Heart's Bunch'.

had this little brass spy-glass an' he was up in the rocks watching what was going on when one of the boys jumped him. We shaved his head. He didn't look so handsome then. And then we ran him out tied back to front on the saddle of his own hoss."

"Oh, Ad!" said Oggie reproachfully.

Sometimes he startled her. She had not known him in those wild days. But deep down he's a good man, she thought, a mighty good man. Should they be running like this? Was this a good thing, the *right* thing? Suddenly she was uncertain and afraid.

But Hardneck, free, riding, seemed to be in tip-top spirits. He pointed. "See them rocks? Shaped like three witches sitting down, squatting round a fire maybe, pointed hats an' all? The camp's in a leetle draw beyond there."

"I always thought them rocks looked like a bunch of horned toads," said Brackburn. "I been here before."

"I know. But Oggie ain't."

"Let us wait till we get there," Oggie said, "and then I'll tell you what I think of the place. I do think myself that those rocks look like a church with spires, put together, a little church."

"Yeh, I see that, honey," said Hardneck.

"Me too," said Brackburn.

They were silent then.

*   *   *

Sometimes the fights took place in large barns or schoolhouses, saloons, gambling halls, even cathouses.

But, most often, if the weather was favourable, they were staged in the open air, in town squares, in meadows adjacent to towns, at barbecues and fairs and as an adjunct to bucking contests and races and the like.

If there was space a ring was not always used and rounds were uneven in length and rules were slack—as long as a man did not bite, or gouge, or kick, he could go ahead and do pretty well anything else that enabled him to put his man down and keep him there. Most fights were fought to a finish, which meant one man unconscious on the boards, the ground, the turf.

It would be true to assert that in the grassy draw which served as a training camp for some of the top fighters, the rules were more strict than they were outside and a man tried to fight 'properly'. A ring was used, and light gloves, and men wore bands around their heads and sometimes guard-muffs over their ears.

Tall Lincrane might have been said to be an 'aristocrat of the bare-knuckle fraternity' and he was indeed top champion now also, in his weight that is. He was, of course, tall—and he was also gangling and he had little body hair (some of the boys looked like apes) and long muscles like pliable ropes. His big nose had been broken so that it was hooked and he had gaps in his teeth which made him look like a cheerful boy, thus fooling some of his opponents all to hell. He had a drooping black moustache and thick long hair which bunched at the back of his neck. He had a way of being gangling at one minute, even shambling, and then, the next, dancing like a rubber-legged monkey, his fists in five different places at once.

That day he was working out with his favourite sparring partner of late, a hardheaded, bull-like pug called Rammer.

Rammer worked like a battering ram, and fast too, so that you could only catch him on the turns. He could make Tall dance all right!

He caught Tall with a really bright one that day— when Tall wasn't looking at him, was looking past him, opening those white and gappy urchin's teeth in a delighted yell.

The yell was cut off in mid-windpipe, as it were, when Rammer's fist, gloved but exceeding heavy, caught Tall on the side of the head and sent him spinning like a champion humming top in a whirling contest.

Tall was forcibly turned towards the people he had been about to greet so joyfully and he finished on his knees, looking up at them, shaking his head, his black locks falling over his eyes. Even his grin had been knocked lop-sided.

The big bearded man climbed through the ropes, reached down and grabbed Tall's smaller paw in his huge one and hauled him to his feet. They shook hands vigorously, while with his free hand Tall moved his jaw around experimentally.

The young man with the rifle who had waylaid the new-come trio asked, "Do you know these people, Mister Lincrane?"

"Of course I know 'em, you jackass. Why do you

think I'm shaking this big ape's paw? Ain't you never heard of Hardneck Gordino?"

"Oh, yeh. I—I'm sorry, Mister Gordino."

"That's all right, son."

The redfaced younker went back to his post.

"He's a new fish," said Tall. He looked over Hardneck's shoulder. "Oggie. Brackburn."

They answered him cheerfully. Everybody was cheerful. Rammer called, "Did you see that punch, Hardneck? Wasn't it a beaut?"

"It was, Rammer, it purely was."

"He caught me while I wasn't looking," said Tall. "I was staring at your ugly mug. I thought I was seeing things."

"Stars, that's what you wuz seein'," jibed Rammer.

* * *

The sun was getting very hot and there was a blueish sort of haze ahead of them, and the soft thud of their horses' hooves was the only sound that broke the stillness. That and the jingling of bridles and the creak of leather. They were both taciturn men. They were not talking now.

Besides their two horses they had Jake Boots' pack-mule which he would use to haul back his supplies from the town called Balkan.

The plains around here were flat, the ground hard and brittle, the grass sparse and coarse. It was not good grazing or growing land. After they had passed the sweet spring of which Boots had earlier spoken the terrain got rockier, and the spring itself disappeared in a cluster of rocks or, rather, bubbled up out of the earth beneath them.

They had replenished their canteens at the spring, the water there being much fresher than the staler stuff—though it had come from the same source originally—which they had brought from the ghost town which had once been called No Hope. Now they began to climb a little. But these were not hills, they were mere rocky lumps. This was where the gold had been in the old days. Ahead of them was a grove of thin-looking cottonwoods, the first substantial signs of vegetation they had seen for miles.

Boots opened his mouth as if to say something. Maybe he had been about to suggest they now show a modicum of caution. But the sound he made—the lips stretching wider in a rictus of shock—was like a loud, breathy sob.

The crack of the rifle was like something in the air, not seeming to come from any particular direction.

Boots bent in the saddle, as if he had stomach cramps and was riding that way in order to alleviate these. But then he pitched forwards against his horse's neck and slid around it. He fell from the saddle in a sort of slow motion, face forward, and then downwards. He hit the ground, however, in a sort of ball and lay still, curled up, his knees bent deeply. His hat, which had not fallen off, covered his eyes.

Amos Crowle was out of the saddle much more quickly and lying flat on his belly, his gun out. He reached forth with his free hand and tilted the hat backwards on Boot's head.

There was death in the old and contorted face, the blankly staring eyes.

Crowle's horse screamed as the rifle sounded again. The beast fell sideways, suddenly boneless. Crowle had to scramble out of the way. The horse fell between Crowle and the body of the old man.

The beast was still alive, its head turned towards Crowle, the big eyes full of an uncomprehending and beseeching agony.

"Oh, Christ," said the man softly.

He pointed his gun at the beast's head and fired one shot.

ELEVEN

The dust had settled on the dead. Two more rifle-shots, fired from the clump of cottonwoods, obviously the only good cover nearby, had failed to find Crowle out. He was protected by the body of the horse, his friend in life, and now in death.

Old Boots' horse and the pack mule were a distance away, finding grass, the shooting not bothering them anymore.

With his hand-gun Crowle fired a couple of shots at the cottonwoods, but realised he was a mite out of range. His rifle was trapped in its scabbard beneath the body of the horse. The two shots were a vain attempt to flush out the marksman. There was a wide-open space between Crowle and the trees, a space as flat as a barroom floor, as perilous as a wild, thick patch of prickly pear and Spanish bayonet.

Boots had had a premonition, Crowle thought; the old man had figured that Max Railham might still be around. But he had not paid enough heed to that premonition, and neither had Crowle, a bit impatient maybe with the rambling of the ancient near-hermit.

Railham must have spotted Crowle, have put two and two together and come up with five. Then, like the professional he was, he had not come into No Hope, he had waited for them to come out. The cottonwoods had been a dandy night bivouac and an even dandier ambuscade spot by day.

This man would never come out into the open, never meet his opponent face to face, not if he could help it. He was as deadly as a rattlesnake waiting in the shadows, not coming out into the sun until it was time to strike, preferably from behind. This was a killer who only killed for money, or, if forced to do so, for his own protection. This was a killer who liked the shadows and the night. But Crowle did not underestimate him. This was a killer who was a professional.

But this was a man, a city fox who did not carry with him the pride that many Western professionals did; this was a man who would run when he felt he had to run.

He ran now. Crowle only had a fleeting glimpse of him, galloping his horse out of the shelter of the cottonwoods, on the other side. Even with a long gun it would have been a ticklish shot. And Railham and his mount soon disappeared from view.

By dint of pushing and pulling, and with more than a modicum of grunting and cursing, Crowle managed to move the dead horse enough to be able to get the saddle off its back and the Winchester repeater with its scabbard. He rounded up Boots' horse, an elderly rawboned beast, but worthy. The saddle was not much good and he replaced it with his own. He took Boots' old Sharps and his belt-gun, an equally ancient Paterson.

Regretfully he had to leave his own horse behind—there was nothing else he could have done.

He put the old man's body over the back of the mule and climbed onto the horse, taking the lead rope.

The little cortège skirted the grove of spindly cottonwoods. There was no sign of the fleeing killer now, just the flat plain once more, the sun, the heat haze. Amos Crowle was sunk in a sort of melancholy as he rode steadily on. His head had begun to ache and he knew his bandage needed changing again.

* * *

Tall Lincrane said: "Jacko Rooney is here. He wants me to join up with him."

Hardneck Gordino said: "And what are you going to do?"

"I'm still thinking about it."

"Jacko's got a good team. But it's all sort of circus-like isn't it?"

"Yeh, that's what I'm thinking about."

They sat outside an old Army tent of mottled brown canvas. Hardneck, Tall, Oggie, Brackburn. Tall's sparring partner, Rammer, was making coffee at a fire nearby.

There were other tents and one lopsided frame building, looking like a ranch bunkhouse—and serving as the same sometimes—which was a sort of communal meeting place. Even when there were not any tents pitched in the area there was always somebody at the house as a sort of caretaker, not always the same person or people but ostensibly the occupant or occupants, having an answer for any curious pilgrim who happened along.

There was a fair number of people here today, a fair amount of tents, and men sat in the shade outside the house. There were a few women moving about. One of them waved to the newcomers and Oggie waved back.

"There's Rooney," said Tall.

The man stood in the doorway of the house and he seemed to be watching them, though he did not nod, make a sign, raise a hand in greeting.

He was medium-sized but with big shoulders and a barrel chest, thus seeming topheavy. His head was almost hairless. He was not wearing a hat. His face was paler than the faces of the men around him and he was clean-shaven. It was a face that looked as if it had been lived in and lived in hard. But it was a face that, with the guileless pale eyes, gave nothing away.

Jacko Rooney was an ex-sergeant who had had a fine record fighting for the South in the war between the states. He now ramrodded a travelling prizefighting team which he called Rooney's Fight-to-a-Finish Brigade. He ran his troupe the way he had run his squad during the war but with the added flamboyancy—in his Army days he would not have countenanced this—of a disciplined circus. He was a good showman.

Still without really acknowledging that he had seen them, Rooney left his doorway and began to walk towards the group that held Tall Lincrane and his new-come friends. He was bowlegged and his arms were long. He did not wear riding boots but ordinary flat-heeled shoes—cowboys would refer to them as 'store shoes'. He walked lightly, springily. It was evident that he could have marched many miles in that fashion. He wore no outer vest and his great chest strained the buttons of his faded Army shirt.

"He's got somep'n in mind," Tall Lincrane said. "That ol' brain-box of his is working again."

*   *   *

It was late night when Sheriff Ep Leary and his two disgruntled deputies returned wearily to Lazy Bend. Doc Pierson was the first to see them. The lanky medico had been worried about his old friend, Ep. He was an old horse travelling the danger trail with two jackasses, deputies Jigger and O'Sanderson.

Ep said Hardneck and his party had vanished. No trail, nothing. You couldn't ride forever. Besides, forever was way out of his jurisdiction. It was a feeble joke and nobody laughed.

Doc Pierson said: "I thought Hardneck was innocent anyway."

"Why did he bust jail then?"

"He didn't do it all on his lonesome, did he? He was busted. Hell, you can't keep a man like Hardneck caged like an animal.''

"What's Amos Crowle gonna say when he gets back?"

"To hell with Amos Crowle," said the lanky doctor. "He ain't God. Besides, he might not even come back. You cross that bridge after it's built, old friend."

Jigger and O'Sanderson did not say anything. They were all out of vengeful talk. They didn't care if Hardneck and his missus and his friend escaped all the way to South America. All they wanted to do was get their heads down and sleep. That old goat of a lawman seemed to be made of wire, but even he seemed kind of frazzled right now.

If this was law-jobbing, Jigger and O'Sanderson thought, they sure as hell didn't want any more of it.

"The morning will bring a new day," Doc Pierson said.

Another half-crazy old goat!

*　　*　　*

It was late when Crowle rode into Balkan on Jake Boots' horse with Jake Boots' body over the back of Jake's old mule as it trailed behind.

During their short time together, Boots had told Crowle that the only person he knew quite well in Balkan was the local storekeeper—a feller called Hanney—who kept the emporium where he (Jake) got his supplies. Hanney, it seemed, was a man of many parts and catered for other needs of the folks of Balkan and its environs. He was barber, undertaker, vet, gunsmith—and he sold hooch on the side, though not for consumption on the premises.

The emporium was at this end of town, Boots had said, so he didn't have to have any truck with other townsfolk if he didn't want to, and he wasn't keen. Besides, Hanney was, like Boots, a lifelong bachelor and lived alone. He was not as old as Boots but he had been around. Sometimes Boots stayed to chew the fat and take a drink on the house before returning to No Hope with his supplies and a spare bottle or two of rye. It was certainly not the best whisky to be got—as Crowle could now testify—but, like baccy, it filled a gap, and Boots had needed to fill that gap.

Well, the poor old jasper would not have to bother his head about filling any more gaps, Crowle thought. He had liked the man. Even though Boots had tried to shoot him down and he (Crowle) still had a headache to prove it!

And the horse too! Crowle had liked that horse.

He'd stomp that murderous snake Railham if it was the last thing he ever did!

A light still shone in the emporium, though not in the shop proper but, warmly, in the back. Crowle moved along the front of the shop and found an alley and steered his mount up there, the loaded mule bringing up the wake. Light came from a curtained window and there was a narrow door.

Crowle dismounted. He rapped upon the door.

He heard shuffling footsteps, and then a voice called, "Who's there?"

"I'm a friend of Jake Boots. I bring bad news."

There was the sound of a key being turned in a lock. The door squealed as it opened stiffly. A doleful face looked out.

"What's this about Jake Boots?"

"He's dead. He's been shot. I've got him here, over the back of his own mule."

"Oh, mercy! Who are you?"

"I'm a lawman. My name is Amos Crowle."

"Seems like I heard that name someplace."

"That's likely. Are you gonna keep me standing out here all night?"

The doleful face withdrew and the door was opened wider.

"You hold the door now," said Crowle, "and I'll bring Jake in."

"Surely, Mr Crowle."

Hanney did as he had been told. He did not ask any more questions, obviously realising now that he wouldn't get any answers anyway, not until the man called Crowle was good and ready.

Crowle came back, carrying the body of Jake Boots as if it were a doll.

"I've got a place for corpses," Hanney said. "But that ain't the place for ol' Jake. Put him on that horse-hair sofa, mister." He had a face like a miserable horse and a mane of gingery-grey hair to match.

Crowle laid Boots' body gently on the sofa.

He straightened, turned. "Seen any strangers in town today?" His tone was peremptory.

Hanney looked startled and worried all at the same time. Then he began to slowly shake his head from side to side.

"No-o, I ain't seen no strangers. Who shot Jake, mister? Was it strangers?"

"One stranger. He'd probably be wearing a brown derby hat and spectacles."

Hanney looked at the lawman as if he suspected he might be slightly mad.

"I ain't seen no man with a brown derby. I would remember if I had. Nobody new in spectacles either."

"Sure, you'd remember. You got any coffee, Mr Hanney?"

The voice was less sharp now.

"I didn't know you knew my name."

"Jake Boots told it me."

"Oh! Yeh, I'll fix some coffee, Mr Crowle."

TWELVE

Crowle came out of Hanney's place by the same way that he had gone in. The horse and the mule were still patiently waiting and he figured it was time he took them down to the livery stables, which Hanney had told him was only a few doors away, going into town. He was not usually so remiss with the livestock which, like all travelling Westerners, he needed so much.

He had put Hanney in the picture as much as he could, without wasting time. The old man was slower on the uptake than his friend Boots had been, but he was likeable, and loyal. And now he was sad. Jake Boots was in good hands.

It was the horse that warned Crowle, by giving vent to an explosive snort. The man's senses were tuned to a fine pitch. He did not think, did not have time to—he merely *reacted*. He whirled and dropped. The ground was uneven and he went down awkwardly, but his gun was in his hand.

The man in the shadows fired two shots rapidly. Originally they had obviously been intended for

Crowle's back. They went over his head. The alley was full of reverberating echoes, gunsmoke, the smell of cordite, sharp, biting to the throat and the nostrils. An animal screamed. It sounded like the mule behind Crowle. The man on the ground fired two retaliatory shots, a rolling noise that caught up the echoes and intensified them, rolled them along the alley like thunder. Another man screamed and Crowle grinned wolfishly. But he thought he heard running footsteps, if it were not a trick of the echoes.

He rolled, flattened himself against the wall in a half-crouching position. No shots tried to find him out. He fired one more shot. But if there had been a shape up there in the blackness—he could not even be sure that he had *seen* a shape—there did not seem to be anything there now.

Crowle rose and, still hugging the wall, ran lightfooted to the end of the alley. The echoes had died and, above the small sounds of his own approach, Crowle heard the footsteps again. There was a pause and then the sound of horses-hooves, the beat quickening.

Crowle turned out of the alley and he was out back of town, the plains breezes blowing in his face, but nothing particularly cooling about them.

He could see nothing moving. The hoofbeats quickly died in the night. Behind him somebody started to shout. His gun still in his hand, Crowle turned about and retraced his steps. He went warily. When he got to the mouth of the alley he called softly, "Mr Hanney."

"I'm here, Mr Crowle." Hanney it seemed did not scare easily—he could have been sticking his neck out.

He was in his doorway, a shotgun in his hands.

Crowle said: "Some bastard tried to drygulch me. I'm going after him. I reckon he's hit. One of the beasts is hit. I hope it's not the horse."

"I'll get a lantern." The old man went back into his abode, returned quickly with a lantern, and the alley was bathed in light.

It was the mule that had been hit, but it was a superficial wound, a red score across his neck.

"I'll fix him," said Hanney.

"I'll take the horse. Do you mind if I take along also Boots' old Sharps?"

"Not at all, Mr Crowle. I reckon Jake would mebbe want you to have it. That's a powerful, *reaching* weapon. I'll go get it." Hanney handed the lantern to Crowle and went back indoors. He soon returned with the heavy long gun, and cartridges.

Crowle handed the lantern over and climbed into the saddle. He took the Sharps.

The town was coming awake. "You better talk to the people," Crowle said. "I'll get along."

"Leave it to me, Mr Crowle. Take care now."

"I will. *Adios*."

"*Vaya con Dios, amigo*."

It was the old border farewell, the old prayer. And Hanney sounded as if he meant it.

Amos Crowle rode once more out into the night.

He had not realised it would take him so long to get wind of his man. Maybe the man was not as badly wounded as had been thought, maybe he had made more noise about it than had been warranted. A sudden bullet from the dark was a mighty scarey thing, like a redhot blow with an invisible missile.

Dawn came. Although Crowle had refilled his two canteens back in Balkan he had not picked up any supplies. He had not had time. He reined in the horse, and took a pull at his canteen. He dismounted, took off his kerchief and soaked it in water and laved the horse's nostrils and mouth. Old Boots had picked this beast well. He was no racer and his age was kind of indeterminate. But he was tough and steady. He was thirsty, but he did not seem at all tired.

As they paused, the sky lightened in front of them and there was a redness as the sun began to poke tentative fingers into the morning.

Crowle thought he thought he saw something moving, way off in the distance.

It was there. Then it was gone.

Crowle shaded his eyes with his hand. The plain seemed to go on forever. But the man knew that, as the morning light grew and the sun became stronger he would be able to see into infinity. Until the sun really reached the apex of its power and the heat intensified and heat-haze grew, became a blue mist, cutting off the far horizon once more.

Crowle got once more into the saddle. "Go, boy," he said, remembering how he used to talk to his old horse.

If that moving thing ahead was Max Railham . . .

"Go, boy!"

But perhaps the moving thing had been only a mirage — though it *was* a bit early for mirages.

Then, as the light got brighter, he saw the thing again.

Maybe it was only a lost maverick.

But it looked like a man on a horse.

*   *   *

Early that morning Jacko Rooney's Fight-to-a-Finish Brigade crossed the New Mexico border into Texas. It was a veritable caravan, almost a waggon-train, if smaller than they used to be in the old days when the Indians were on the rampage and there was a measure of safety in greater numbers.

But there *had* been massacres in this very area, for, in the main, the waggon-people had not been fighting people. There were not many warlike Indians around in this area now, though the Apaches still rampaged from time to time on the other side of Texas where the Rio Grande separated it from Mexico. Wild Indians would not have fazed this bunch much, however, for they *were* fighting people. Also they had two extra recruits that they had picked up at the training camp. Hardneck Gordino and Tall Lincrane, both pastmasters in the art of gunplay as well as in the art of fisticuffs.

And that was not all. Hardneck had his lusty blonde missus with him and she was handy with a long gun, and Hardneck had his old 'manager' along too, Brackburn. Fists or guns—they were both grist to that old rustler and Indian-fighter's particular mill.

Rooney had gotten himself three good men and one good woman. He had a sneaking idea that the trio was on the run from something. But he knew them from old. And, besides, he had made it his policy never to ask personal questions. Rooney had persuaded Tall— whom he had been after anyway—and Tall and Hardneck had got their heads together and the big blackbearded fighter had volunteered to come along too, providing of course that he could bring Oggie and Brackburn. Fine, said Jacko Rooney, a pleased look in his pale eyes.

Oggie was not the only woman along, of course, Many of the men had wives or women friends along with them. Any filly was welcome as long as she did not cause trouble among the men. They were fighting animals and they needed their oats from time to time. Sometimes one or the other of them picked up a filly in one of the towns where bouts were put on and toted her along. But, if she played fast and loose, she was dumped from the train quicker than any chopped-nose Apache squaw could be banished from her tribe.

Rooney liked Hardneck's missus, despite the funny way she talked. Hell, he was Irish himself and when he got real mad he sounded like his old man used to when he had 'the devils' from rotten booze. There would be no shennanigans with Miz Oggie. She was a straight lady right along the line. Besides, any man try anything with her, Hardneck would tear the head off him.

Rooney had been after Tall and Hardneck for his 'brigade' for a long time. Now, although he made great pains not to show it, he was a man who right now was mighty pleased with himself.

*   *   *

The light was getting better. But the sun was in Crowle's eyes.

He seemed to be getting nearer to his man though.

Yes, he was sure now that the moving thing ahead was a man. And a horse. A man on a horse.

The air was like a hot and furry blanket so that a man feared that if he took a deep breath he might choke on the stuff that went into his throat and lungs. A man took small breaths and tried not to exert himself too much, sitting still in the saddle, letting the horse carry him along. But Crowle set his mount at a steady jog and was inevitably bounced in the saddle rather more than somewhat. He blinked the sweat from his eyes. It ran like warm and sticky oil down his spine.

He was gaining though, he was sure he was gaining.

Then he saw something happen. He saw the rider ahead of him fall out of the saddle, a little figure like a doll falling from a toy rocking horse. He pushed his own mount. 'Go, boy!'. But the little figure was up again, then was part of the horse once more.

Is it Railham, thought Crowle, is it? Has he been wounded bad, or is he passing out from lack of water? Still a tenderfoot, Jake Boots had called him. Was it

Railham? Who else could it be?

Something was driving Crowle now. He realised that it was cold, murderous rage. But the sardonic humour that had always kept him sane lurked in the back of his mind with a crooked, devil's grin. Say if that wasn't Railham after all, but some weary, sick, thirsty pilgrim whose trail had passed across that of the killer and his hunter.

But then the man ahead halted his horse and got down from the saddle.

Crowle did not know what the man was about—until he heard the distant crack of the rifle, a puny thing in the hot air. He did not hear the slug. Goddamit, he thought, the stupid jackass is out of range!

He climbed down from his own horse and took the loaded Sharps from across the front of the saddle. He got down on one knee and raised the heavy fifty-calibre gun to his shoulder. Buffalo hunters used this because of its long range. Crowle wished that he had a rest of the kind that these hunters used. Pastmasters at that type of slaughter killed a lot of buffaloes in a day's work and a rest of some kind—even a stout cleft branch from a tree—was of great help. But there was not a tree for miles on this arid plain where Crowle rested now.

The man up ahead tried another shot and there was a puff of sand from the ground a few yards ahead of Crowle. The man was getting better. He had a good gun, maybe a Winchester, and he was using it well.

Crowle drew a bead on the black figure and squeezed the trigger of the big gun.

He had anticipated the recoil but, even so, it rocked him. How could a man shoot all day with one of these blunderbusses, for God's sake? But the barrel was so long it looked slender and the bullet spun along it at high velocity—Crowle almost thought he heard it hum. He saw the figure become foreshortened and the report of the gun seemed to roll backwards, almost as if being sucked back into that long barrel.

The black figure became still. It seemed a lot smaller.

Crowle remained low down and waited and watched. Up ahead the horse began to move desultorily away from the still figure.

Crowle climbed back onto his own horse, lugging the Sharps with him.

He wondered whether he had acted prematurely. If that was Railham up there he had not wanted to kill him. He had wanted to find out whether the man had been actually hired and, if so, who had hired him.

But hell, the man had been shooting at him, hadn't he? When folks shot at him, he shot back, by cracky he did—that was the principle. And at that range, even with a long-reacher like the Sharps, a man could not pick his spot to hit. He might have got his target plumb through the head.

With the Sharps across the saddle in front of him he rode his horse slowly forward.

THIRTEEN

Jigger and O'Sanderson had resigned their posts. They had also left Lazy Bend. Sheriff Ep Leary was glad to see the back of them and hoped he would never have to look at them again, back or front. He had had some deputies in his day, but those two had surely been the most inept—he couldn't think why he had countenanced them in the first place.

What help would those two barflies have been if they had caught up with Hardneck and his missus and old Brackburn? Now, Ep was kind of glad that they hadn't. Maybe, as Doc Pierson had said, Hardneck was innocent anyway. Hardneck had gone! Amos Crowle had gone! Things were back to normal. Folks soon forgot . . .

But Ep felt uneasy, felt he was still waiting for something . . .

What did he think he ought to do—go after Hardneck and the others all on his lonesome? Doc Pierson had told him he was an idiot, maybe needed dosage of some kind.

Ep stayed put, or seemed to. At least, he did not leave town. But he was as restless as a mule with a boil in its ass.

And Doc Pierson could not really give him anything for that, not his restlessness.

Doc had told him that he always did worry too much. But Ep Leary was kind of an old hoss now and he could not change his nature. He waited, he worried, he fidgeted . . .

But, now, although Ep did not know it, Amos Crowle was getting some answers.

*   *   *

It was not a large Texas town but the grass around it was good and there were some small ranches and farms and a spread that supplied horses for rodeo work.

This particular undertaking actually ran a rodeo of its own once a year and, with time, this had become a gala occasion; and, apart for the roughriders and the bulldoggers and the like, other acts were welcome, including Jacko Rooney's Fight-to-a-Finish Brigade.

And the challengers came too.

And the confidence tricksters and the bunco artists and the shills and the whores in all their finery and the patent-medicine men and the trick-shooters and the rundown circus acts and the drummers selling all kinds of wares and, this year, even a sword-swallower and a fat lady with a very thin man who was tattooed from top to toe—until a bunch of cowboys threw him into the local creek and the coloured paint peeled away.

Nobody bothered to shoot him. It was all good fun, an annual holiday for all.

Leastways, everybody managed to get away for some part of the day to sample his or her particular likes.

By now bare-knuckle prizefights were firm favourites, even with the females who in the beginning had clucked with dismay at the sight of so much hairy male flesh, so much brutish masculinity.

*   *   *

It was Tall Lincrane who thought of the new slant on Hardneck—not even 'Hardneck', who had been out of the game for some time. No; Bruno, the Hooded Bear! That was near the bone maybe, for Hardneck had once fought a grizzly bear and had the scars to prove it and a nickname that would stay with him for life. But Jacko Rooney—still not asking any questions—well, he liked the name. And Oggie and Brackburn did not actually turn their noses up at it.

They put on an exhibition bout. That popular beanpole Tall Lincrane and the mysterious Bruno, the Hooded Bear—who, as given out by Jacko in his introductory peroration, came from a strange land beyond the seas and when unmasked was a fearsome sight to look upon.

As it was, the Bear wore a black hood with slits cut out for his eyes and nostrils and mouth. The wide bottom of this came almost to the man's mighty shoulders and, between this and his waist he was stripped bare. His chest was barrel-like and matted with black hair. He had no fat at his middle and his arms were roped with muscle. He wore black shorts and his legs, though not thin, looked fast, moving on surprisingly small feet. He was almost as tall as his opponent—Tall himself—and a hell of a lot broader.

For this bout, which was a friendly one, they used light gloves. They were both stylish. They were well-matched. But, slowly, Tall began to get the upper hand, slowly driving his opponent back. The crowd loved this. They went wild. The women screeched. They liked Tall, a perfect gentleman when he was not fighting. The hooded hairy man—a veritable giant—made them shudder in their frilly pantaloons.

It was skilfully done, the way the two men fought, the way Tall got the upper hand. Although the crowd could not have suspected it, this was all a preliminary for what was to follow.

The fight was at an end. As it had been a friendly one, no verdict was given. But there was no doubt who the crowd's winner was, their champion. Tall Lincrane bowed to tumultuous applause. The Hooded Bear stood by with drooping shoulders and dangling arms.

Then Jacko Rooney pulled the next rabbit out of the hat. The Hooded Bear would fight anybody to a finish, no gloves, prize-money on the nail.

Professional, semi-professional, ambitious amateur, the challengers came forth. That hooded gink, despite his looks, was no great potatoes!

The fallen man was Max Railham.

His brown derby lay in the brown grass beside him. One lens of his spectacles was starred, obscuring his eye, making it strange at least. His other eye looked up at Crowle with an uncomprehending stare.

The bullet fired from the Sharps rifle had got the man in the thigh. Thick blood pumped from an artery. He had been hit before though, obviously at the end of the alley in the town called Balkan. He had been hit high up in the chest, between the shoulder and the heart, and his clothing was caked with blood.

It was a miracle he had got this far. He had run like a scared and hurt animal. He was dying.

Crowle got down on one knee before him, moving the Winchester to one side in order to do so. Railham had made a good try with that Winchester. He had remained a professional till the last. But Crowle did not like professionals who shot people in the back.

Crowle said: "Who hired you to kill Ryley and Bick in Lazy Bend?"

Railham was younger than Crowle had expected him to be. He bared his teeth, revealing a broken one in the almost boyish face.

"I'm finished, aren't I?"

"You're finished all right," Crowle told him. "I was gonna blow your head off anyway. You killed Jake Boots. You killed my horse."

Railham gave a little spurt of laughter. Blood ran out of his mouth and down his chin. He coughed. The blood ran faster. "I was shooting at you," he said. The words made a burbling sound.

"Who hired you?"

"What if I tell you I did the job for myself?"

"I wouldn't believe you. I *do not* believe you. Not you."

"Lemmy Spring hired me."

"I figured Lemmy Spring would have something to do with it. Why did he hire you?"

"Give me some water."

"It won't do you any good."

"It isn't going to do me much harm now, is it?"

Crowle rose to his feet. He went to Railham's own horse, which had not wandered too far away, and got the canteen from the saddle and took it back to the man and gave him what he wanted. It ran down his chin, thinning the blood. Railham coughed. There was water with the blood.

He let the canteen fall. He had held it himself, but he could not hold it any longer.

"You're Amos Crowle?"

"I am."

"I saw you before. It was a long time ago. We did not speak or anything."

He talks like an educated man, thought Crowle. But it was time he talked turkey.

"Why did Lemmy Spring want Ryley and Bick dead?"

"They were the only people who could identify him. Except me." Railham stretched his lips in a death's grin. He could not laugh anymore. "Maybe he'll want me dead now."

"You're cheating on him then, aren't you? Tell me more."

"Lemmy is living in the Pecos country under an assumed name. He's married and has a kid. He's building up a small ranch . . ." Railham's words were becoming halting. "He had a fancy doctor do something to his face. You wouldn't know him . . . A-aah . . ."

"The name, man, the name?"

"Summer . . . Caleb Summer . . ."

Lemmy Spring. Caleb Summer. From Spring to Summer. Lemmy—now Caleb—obviously had a sense of humour anyway.

Max Railham was dead.

Crowle had had the best of the story, but not the whole of it. Would he ever find out now, he wondered, how those two saddle tramps, Ryley and Bick, had discovered that Spring was now Summer?

He had a hell of a lot more travelling to do. Yes, he meant to finish this job, finish it completely, long haul or no long haul.

The Pecos River country of Texas was a long haul indeed from here. And, even when he got there, to that big territory, he still had to find a ranch which belonged to a man called Caleb Summers who had a wife and a child.

A man whose face he would have known but now would not recognise anymore . . .

He left Max Railham for the buzzards and took his

horse and gear. He would need a spare horse. Railham had had no food, and very little water. He had very little money either. He obviously had not collected his pay.

Yes, Mr Spring-Summer would only pay by results, no doubt.

Here I come, Mr Spring-Summer, Crowle thought, sooner or later, a payee who deals in lead.

He wondered how far was the next town.

"Go, boy."

*   *   *

Tall Lincrane always fought in his bare feet.

No, that was not strictly true. He wore mocassins when working out at the training camp, just as he wore light gloves. And he had worn both mocassins and gloves for his 'exhibition bout' with Bruno, the Hooded Bear.

As they moved from town to town, from settlement to settlement, sometimes putting on a show at a ranch or mine, the exhibition bout became a regular thing. And then came the challengers for the Bear—and opponents for Tall and others of Jacko Rooney's Fight-to-a-Finish Brigade.

The Bear took on all comers, and beat them. And the word got around, and the exhibition bout, which was basically just a come-on, had to be abandoned. And the good pros began to come forward and challenge the Bear, and his fame grew, for he beat most of these also.

It was inevitable that the real identity of Bruno, the Hooded Bear, should become known among the sporting fraternity, and old opponents, old friends of Hardneck Gordino (a man who had actually fought a bear) began to come forward to renew acquaintanceship and to test him in his new guise.

* * *

Amos Crowle crossed the border between New Mexico and Texas at a different spot to the 'brigade' who had gone before him, many many miles away—it was a long border. He did not know about the Brigade and that Hardneck was with them.

He had debated about returning to Lazy Bend with the story that Max Railham had told him but had soon decided against it. It would take too much time. He would have to get on, to do it his way.

As for Hardneck, he was a grown man and a tough one. For the time, he would have to put up with what he had.

Had he known that Hardneck was now not nearly so far away, was free, things might have been different. But, man of many talents that he was, Amos Crowle was not blessed with the second sight.

He also did not know that, in a sense, he was being anticipated . . .

PART TWO

Texas—Retribution

FOURTEEN

Caleb Summer—who used to be Lemmy Spring—was
a tall, middle-aged stoop-shouldered man with a badly
scarred face, parallel lines down his cheeks as if he had
been marked by Indians. There were small grooves
under his eyes too and the eyes themselves were very
deep set and could look at a person so wildly sometimes
that that person became afraid.

He looked like a man who had seen much trouble and
was trying to forget. He looked like a man, too, who was
used to having his own way, or always meant to get it.

Like most Westerners he wore a hat continually. If
without it, he was seen to be going bald, his remaining
hair dark and flecked with grey, his brow and his bald
patches having dark patches on them like stains.

His chin, his lips and his nose were good. Maybe he
had once been a handsome man.

Whether or not, he had certainly captured a
beautiful woman for his wife. She was dark. She might
have had Mexican or Indian blood, but nobody
wondered aloud about this in the presence of her

husband. Her hair was thick and raven black and worn to her shoulders, merely tied back with a ribbon, tempering its wildness. It went well with the large, deep-brown eyes beneath it, and a serene brow, high, white, tinged with a delicate olive. Her face was exquisitely formed with a straight nose, lips that were full, red, finely chiselled, a chin that was of just the right proportion to match the rest of her features and had a small dimple, like a hole poked with a little finger, giving a girlish look to that patrician face.

The neck was beautifully-moulded and the figure beneath, always simply but cunningly adorned, was something to make a man's heart pound—high, full breasts, small waist flowing to flawless hips and tight buttocks and long legs as muscular and supple as a fighting cat's.

Her name was Lola.

This was the woman Caleb Summer had brought with him to this place. She was plumper then, and the neighbourhood women told their husbands why this was so. Then, months later, she bore Caleb a child, a chubby dark boy who had his mother's beauty and his father's smouldering temper.

The Summer's had taken over the old Painter place. Joe Painter had been dead close on twelve months and the spread deteriorating. Ma Painter had been glad to sell.

Joe Painter had had cows and horses but no recognisable brand. Behind his back folks said he was a handy man with a running iron and a maverick-stealer from way back. But nobody had ever proved anything.

Such things could not be said about the new owner of 'Painter's Place'. He chose a brand. He called the place the Rainbow Ranch and the brand looked like a horseshoe that somebody had tried to bend straight and had not quite made it—it looked like a rainbow. It wasn't a particularly easy brand to do, even with a running iron.

Summer had five hands now, whereas the Painters had only had two, and they a couple of dead-beats who quit as soon as the old man died. Summer picked good cowhands, three of whom were known in the area.

Then the sixth man came.

He professed to be a cowhand too. But he was different to the others.

You only had to look at him.

He was young and lean and he wore black clothes which made him look sleek. They were not what you might call 'store clothes', but neither were they the sort of clothes you expected a working ranny to wear either.

He could rope though, and he could ride. He was the best. But he never seemed to get dirty. He was like a sleek, fast black cat who licked himself constantly.

His name was Parley Masters.

He wore twin pearl-handled forty-five calibre Peacemaker Colts. Like a sharpshooter in a circus, some folk might have said. But others recognised the stamp of this young man and they walked small around him.

Caleb Summer knew him best. Caleb Summer had

hired him. But not specifically for a cowhand. He did not need any more cowhands. Not yet.

He *would* need them. He meant to need them. He meant this to be the biggest ranch in the territory. The Rainbow. Best grazing land. Best water. Best beef. Good hands, whom he didn't mind paying the best *dinero*. A far-reaching prosperous spread. His spread, his and Lola's and the boy's.

And nothing must be allowed to stay in the way of that.

He had made his name in another way. Under another name. *Lemmy.* Lemmy Spring was dead. There was a new man. Caleb Summer. A different man. But a man just as ruthless, a man who would have *his* way.

He said to Parley Masters, "He should be back soon. Max Railham. You can't miss him. He wears spectacles and a brown derby hat. But don't sell him short. He's no figure of fun. If he shoots at you he won't miss. But he likes things easy, a shot from the dark, a shot in the back. I don't think he can out-draw you. But you've got to make it good. Self-defence. I want no kick-backs."

"Leave it to me, Mr Summer."

"He'll hit town first. He's got to come that way."

"I'll keep my ears peeled back and my eyes wide open, Mr Summer."

When Railham came back, Ryley and Bick would be dead, Summer knew that. That back-shooting pantywaist, Railham, was very conscientious about fulfilling his 'commissions', as he called them. He was proud of his expertise and what a Westerner would

have called his 'rep'. He was the only man left who
knew that Caleb Summer was really Lemmy Spring.

It was a pity that crook surgeon had made such a
messy job of Lemmy-Caleb's face. He was dead now, of
course, but not before, in his cups, he had blabbed to
Lemmy-Caleb's two old gang-members, Ryley and
Bick, simpletons with big mouths. But Max Railham
would have taken care of them, and their big mouths.
And now Max would get his cumuppance. And that
polite deadly young man who called himself Parley
Masters only knew the man who hired him as Mister
Caleb Summer.

Afterwards, that young man, richer by the *dinero* that
Summer had originally promised to Railham (and
some bonus to boot) could go on his way. Until, if there
were other obstacles, Summer might need him again.

Of course, Summer did not know for certain sure that
Parley Masters could put Railham down.

There were other things that Summer did not know.

He did not know that, although Ryley and Bick had
been taken care of, their assassin, Railham, was dead
also.

He did not know that Amos Crowle was now on the
trail of Spring-Summer. He had one advantage,
however—though he did not know about that either,
that it might occur! He would know Amos Crowle if he
saw him, but Amos Crowle would not know him.

Parley Masters would know Amos Crowle also.

And there was somebody else at the Railbow Ranch who would know Amos Crowle.

*   *   *

And it was that somebody else who saw him first.

FIFTEEN

Lola Canalete was a dance-hall girl in El Paso when she
first met Lemmy Spring.

She was there when Max Railham killed the bank
guards, leaving the way open for Lemmy and the rest of
the boys to take the bank.

Jake Boots had been with them then also. Lola
remembered Jake. A nice old gent. He was probably
dead long since.

She had danced with Lemmy the night before. She
knew who he was. The gang were pretty brazen, there
in town. But nobody had known why they were there,
not till afterwards.

Lemmy had made quite a play for her. He had been a
big handsome man. Devil-may-care. She had been
attracted to him. The danger of him. The animal,
sexual vitality of him.

He had not followed through that night and she
thought she had seen the last of him. But then, almost
as if it had been ordained, she accidentally got in the
way of the riders as, after shooting up the bank—and
part of the town too—they left in a hurry.

She liked riding. She could not afford a horse of her own but hired one from the local livery stable on the mornings when she wanted to go riding.

This was one of those mornings and she was just coming back to town when the gang bore down on her, she was caught up in a maelstrom of horseflesh and dust. And Lemmy's white teeth grinned at her and his mad eagle's eyes shone. He grabbed her reins and turned her horse about and whipped him hard on the flanks with a quirt. And then she was in the middle of them and going like the wind.

She was Lemmy's woman for a few weeks and then the gang fell foul of a posse after pulling a freight office job and were hard-pressed. Lola, who had not been identified, was left behind. Lemmy promised he would pick her up later. She pined for him. She had never thought she would ever pine for a man that much.

Months passed and he did not return, although she heard highly-coloured stories about him. She decided to write him off. But that was not easy.

She was a dance-hall girl again, and there were other men. She had never been so beautiful, but she knew that eventually the life would drag her down. There seemed no escape. Was there any escape either for Lemmy? There was always the sadness when she thought of Lemmy.

He was a thief and a killer. A mad dog, some folks called him. He was an intelligent man, but not quite as others; she had known this. He had never talked to her about his earlier life. Did he steal for the love of stealing? Did he kill for the love of killing? Was the excitement of the owlhoot ways the thing he wanted for all of his life? Would he finish up as an ancient horse-minder like Jake Boots?

But it was not her business anymore, and maybe it never had been. She had been living in a dream of what might be.

But then, about seven months from the first time she had seen him, he returned.

He told her he had not been able to keep away from her.

She was with him when he had his operation. She did not mind what it did to him. It would make him safe. It would make *them* safe. She loved him.

They got married. She became Mrs Caleb Summer. They bought the Rainbow Ranch. They had a child. It was a life she had dreamed of . . .

Sometimes she thought about the old days. Sometimes she was afraid that something from the old days would obtrude, and destroy their peace and prosperity.

She knew that her husband would never really be a *peaceful* man—he was still ambitious, still quite ruthless. But he was gentle with her and with his son. He was a strange, two-faced man. But he was her man. He had a dream too, she knew this. And nothing must be allowed to destroy that dream.

She knew that Caleb—she was used to calling him that now—had had more dealings with Max Railham. She did not like Max Railham. He made her flesh crawl. There was no passion in him, no light, no feeling. But she reasoned that what Railham had been sent to do was important to Caleb, was important to *them*.

Then the other one came. A sort of Max Railham, but with a subtle and deadly difference. Lola knew the stripe of men like Parley Masters, so young, so smooth and well-mannered, and so deadly. He did not make her flesh crawl, but deep down inside of herself she was afraid of Parley as she had never been afraid of Max Railham.

Then again, though, she knew that Caleb would never have hired a man like Parley if he did not have a use for him. And everything and everybody 'used' by Caleb was used for the benefit of Lola and the boy and the ranch, and the dream, in order to bring that dream to a glorious reality and fruition.

Parley Masters was unobtrusively, unfailingly courteous, hardworking, helpful. She learned to accept him as she accepted the other hands who doffed their hats to her and called her 'Miz Summer' and looked up to her as the boss's wife, the 'lady of the house'. *Her* dream had come true already!

Really she wanted nothing more but that warmth and safety.

Then, one morning when she was shopping in the neighbouring small cowtown she met an old acquaintance.

She was coming out of the dry goods store when a deep, soft voice said: "Hallo, Lola."

She turned her head. He was leaning against a hitching post and looking at her, his eyes squinted against the sun. She recognised him immediately, the lean indolence of him, the dark lean face with the bar of black moustache. The sardonic eyes were hidden but he smiled a thin crooked smile.

"Amos Crowle!"

"In the same old flesh."

"It's been a long time." He had startled her. Words came from her without much sense behind them.

"A fair to middling time I guess, Lola. How've you been?"

"All right. You?"

"All right. Didn't expect to see you around here."

"I move around, Amos, you know that." It was as if she were trying to put him off the scent. "I'm living round here now."

Yes, it had been a fair to middling time.

The Sunflower House in Abilene, which had been kept at that time by two friends of Crowle, May Sanclaire and Kate Luten. Crowle had been shot-up, his left hand mutilated.*

Lola noticed now that he still wore a glove on that hand.

She had not stayed long at the Sunflower House. But Crowle had left before she had and she had not seen him since, until now.

She had greeted him like an old friend. But now a chill hand clutched at her breast. What was he doing down on the Pecos? She knew his reputation. He was a manhunter, a killer. He travelled far and it was a

This episode is described in 'The Hands of Amos Crowle', though Lola is not actually mentioned.

wonder that she had not met up with him before in her time.

"You're looking fine, Lola," he said and he had moved a little. His face was out of the sun. He was looking at her straight with his slate-grey eyes. She had seen them cold, as expressionless as a snake's. But now they had a warm light in them as they appraised a warm, voluptuous and very beautiful woman.

"Well, thank you, Amos."

"I purely mean that, Lola."

One thing about Amos Crowle, she thought, he always meant what he said.

He had the reputation for *doing* as he said also.

Did he know who she was now? Did he know she was now married to Caleb Summer who had once been Lemmy Spring? It hardly seemed likely—even that he knew that Spring was now Summer. It had been a well-guarded secret.

But you never knew with a man like Amos Crowle.

There was still a big price on Lemmy Spring's head. Was Amos Crowle bounty-hunting? The dread that had always lurked in the back of Lola's mind threatened to burst forth, that, in some way, she might reveal her fears to this hawk-like man. She fought those fears. She smiled.

"I was shopping."

"So I see. Can I carry your bags?"

"Thank you, Amos."

But she did not want him to see the fine gig she now had, the beautifully-matched horses. As they walked she wished she had not taken up his offer. She said quickly, "Oh, I forgot, Amos—I promised to go see a girl-friend of mine who isn't too well. I've got to go back-aways. I'll take the packages."

"Just as you say, Lola. Maybe we'll meet up again, huh?"

"Maybe." She made her voice sound arch. "Where are you staying?"

"The little hotel." He jerked his thumb back over his shoulder.

"I know. Are you staying in town long?"

"It depends. I'm just moseying around."

Pumping Amos Crowle would be like trying to squeeze water out of solid rocks in the badlands.

She left him hurriedly, as if she was late for her suddenly-remembered appointment, the appointment that never was. She wondered if she had fooled him. She doubted it.

To hell with him, she thought, with a sudden return to the girl she used to be, who had used men, who had not given a damn for any man—until she met Lemmy Spring.

But, as she remembered, she had taken a shine to Amos Crowle too, once upon a time. In some ways Amos and Lemmy (whom she should now call Caleb) were much alike. It was a pity that they were on opposite sides of the fence. But were they? Caleb Summer was not on the opposite side of the fence to lawman Crowle, Marshal Black Heart. If Crowle met Caleb would he accept him for what he was? Had Caleb changed that much?

She hardly knew where she was going, only that she was going in the opposite direction from that compelling man she had just left.

Her heart gave another jolt when she suddenly spotted another now-familiar figure. Parley Masters, Caleb's pet young gunfighter. He had seen her too, and he doffed his hat, mockingly it seemed, although it was possible she had imagined this.

She wondered if Parley had seen her with Amos Crowle. She wondered if Parley knew Crowle. Had the fact that Parley was here in this territory—though as far as she knew he had arrived first—had something to do with the fact that Crowle was here too?

It could be said that they were two of a kind. Parley was working for Caleb. So, could it be said that Parley was on the opposite side of the fence to Crowle? Her thoughts bedevilled her.

She went into a small *cantina* kept by a Mexican woman she knew and where she was always welcome. Caleb had even said she spent too much time there.

But it was time to visit Conchita again. They had coffee and a brandy liqueur that the Mexican woman had managed to get from somewhere—probably from one of her border *bandido* sources. They chatted of inconsequential things and the time passed and then Lola took her leave.

She did not see Parley or Crowle again before she drove the gig out of town. She was soon home.

SIXTEEN

She did not know whether her husband, Caleb had ever had any direct contact with Amos Crowle. But she knew that Caleb must know him or have heard of him. Every owlhooter worth his salt had heard of Black Heart Crowle—it was they who had dubbed him such.

She debated for all the rest of the day whether to tell her husband of Crowle's presence or not. She debated with herself until her head rang with anxiety and the tension. She knew Caleb's wolfish temper. She feared what he might do if he got the idea that Crowle had come after him.

She could not possibly imagine that he knew she had previous knowledge of Crowle, and pretty intimate knowledge at that. Caleb had never taken her for an angel. But he had not taken her for a lawman's plaything either and, old long-looper that he was, might take a pretty jaundiced view of Crowle in the rôle of one of his wife's ex-lovers.

Not that it had been any great thing. Crowle had been May Sanclaire's man, and Lola had been employed by May and her partner, Kate.

Rather, May had been Crowle's woman. For no woman had ever actually *captured* that man. Not to Lola's knowledge anyway. Now she began to realise how little she knew of Crowle and any of his motives. She had known him as an attractive, compelling, virile man, and that was all . . .

From her window, washed now by the redness of the dying sun, she saw Parley Masters return to the ranch. Would he be reporting to Caleb now? Had he seen her with Crowle? Had she left it too late?

She had to give instructions to the housekeeper, a new acquisition called Ma Berghof, about the evening meal. This she would share with Caleb, and for most of the time they would be alone. She would not run to him. She would wait for the warm time, the mealtime, a time they shared, and she would bring up the subject in a casual way. Just in case Parley had seen her with Crowle and had already told Caleb so, she would mention that she had once danced with Crowle—after all, that had been her job, or one of her jobs, and she had met all sorts—and he had remembered her and had spoken to her in town today.

She had met many notorious men—not least of all Lemmy Spring—and Crowle was indeed notorious, a man you *would* remember . . .

She helped Mrs Berghof, whom Caleb called 'Ma', a motherly stout widow-woman who thought her new employers were great. They began to hum together an old ballad often heard on the trail and that, the older

woman said, had been her late husband's particular
favourite.

When Caleb joined her at the long refectory table he
seemed in a particularly cheery mood. But he could
change his colours without warning, she knew that.
She had seen him in a gunfight once, laughing with
amusement as the other man taunted him, until the
man drew and was not fast enough. And Lemmy had
been grim and dark again as he killed him.

I never want those days back, Lola thought, I would
do anything to prevent those days coming back.

She could not wait any longer than the soup. She
said: "I got a surprise today."

Caleb said: "You saw Amos Crowle."

"Yes. Did Parley tell you?"

"He did mention it."

"I saw Parley. I did not know whether he had seen
me with Mr Crowle or not."

"How come you know Mr Crowle?" The voice was
mocking, but not unpleasantly so. He seemed
genuinely interested.

"I danced with him once," she said lightly. "I also
danced once with Bill Hickok in Abilene and I danced a
few times with Bat Masterson who is little more than a
boy."

"Yeh, you've known a lot of desperate characters, I
guess."

"You should know, I guess."

He was silent, seeming to examine this remark.

But his next words came as a surprise to her.

"I want to know what Crowle is doing here."

"It may have nothing to do with you."

"I've got to know. Where is he staying, do you know that?"

"At the hotel."

"Find out what he's doing here. You're the only one who can."

She looked at him and suddenly it seemed as if she was not seeing him. She was not sure what he was proposing.

He was still fighting for his liberty, or his life. A new face was no guarantee of safety. A new face did not make him a new man. Had she thought it would? Had she thought it *had*?

It hadn't, of course, she should have realised that long since. He was still the same ruthless, cynical Lemmy, single-minded to the point of madness, using everybody and everything to try and make himself inviolate and all-powerful.

That was the way he was and that was the way she would have to accept him. "I'll try and find out for you," she said simply, and rose from the table and left the room.

*   *   *

The Rainbow Ranch had its troubles now, its troubled people. Not least among these, strangely enough, was the young gunfighter called Parley Masters.

Parley had spotted Amos Crowle, but he did not think Amos had spotted him. He had seen Amos talking to Miz Summer and that had puzzled and troubled him. Because he did not want to run into Amos he had left town quickly; and quickly he had told his boss, Caleb Summer, what he had seen. Afterwards, he wondered whether he should have done this.

Crowle might only be passing through. But now, knowing of his presence, would Caleb Summer want something done about him? Parley had a fast mind as well as a fast gun. But he knew Summer had hired him for his gun, not for his mind. Therefore, whoever Summer actually was or had been, whatever Summer had to hide, it must be something lawless. Many an ex-owlhooter was taking a new identity and building a ranch or another business on ill-gotten gains.

Parley did not know what Summer had been but he had him pegged as a completely ruthless man . . .

Hell, I'm hired, thought Parley, I'm not in this business for fun, I'm in it for money, and maybe I'll own a ranch someday—and whatever the man who hired me asks me to do, that is what I have to do.

He had never wondered about things so much before, never questioned his own motives. You started to do that in this business and, man, you were dead!

Anyway, maybe what he had thought might happen might after all, never happen. And, despite anything else that Parley might try and tell himself, in his heart of hearts he hoped that it would not happen.

He was not scared of Amos Crowle. He was not scared of any man.

But Crowle he knew, Crowle had once been his

mentor and his friend. Parley probably knew as much about the *real* Amos Crowle, the real man behind the bloody legend of Black Heart than any other man living knew or would ever know . . .

SEVENTEEN

Hardneck Gordino was fighting a man called Whip Delune.

Or, at least, Bruno, the Hooded Bear was fighting said Delune.

The Bear, when he was Hardneck, had heard of Whip before but had never met him in any capacity. Whip was younger, a new fish, but a formidable one with the reputation of a man-eating shark.

He was as tall as the Bear, not so broad and hairy, but slimmer in the waist and with exceptionally long legs which gave him his speed, had earned him his nickname.

Jacko Rooney had organised the bout. A canny old bird, he had never matched the Bear with anybody who had fought Hardneck. The Bear was the Bear.

Whip Delune was another fighting man that Rooney had been trying to inveigle into joining his Brigade, but so far without success. So why not, Rooney thought, match this quicksilver upstart against the Brigade's newest star and see what Whip was really made of?

The venue was a horse ranch in Texas, a place that was often the scene also of some pretty fancy rough-riding and bulldogging. The event had been well-publicised in surrounding territories by strategic fly-posting and word-of-mouth.

The prize-ring was, in fact, the smaller corral, the one where a fractious horse might be kept to keep him away from the other stock until such time he could be broken properly.

This made a bigger ring than was usual, giving plenty of room for two fast men to move about, two big men who were light on their feet, and this would really give them full rein, this was a bout that folks came from far and wide to see, the Bear versus the Whip.

The new star, the mysterious hooded monster of Jacko Rooney's Fight-to-a-Finish Brigade, against a now-famous freelance.

The betting was high.

The corral was swept clean by an old Indian with a twig broom which made patterns in the soil, for the broom was wet and not much dust rose and this soon settled. The crowd waited impatiently for the fighters to appear, to start and really raise the dust. There were ironic cheers when the old Indian left the ring and he sloped his broom over his shoulder and bowed mockingly, grinning with snaggle-teeth.

Nobody was allowed to perch on the top rung of the corral-fence, thus obscuring others' view. The stewards saw to this. Jacko Rooney always had plenty of stewards at hand, mainly made up of boys of his who did not happen to be fighting on that particular day.

On this particular day Tall Lincrane and his friend and sparring partner known as Rammer were part of the stewarding party, and nobody was going to argue with bozoes like them.

The best seats were upturned barrels around the fence, and here and there kitchen chairs for the ladies, and folks stood behind them and then there were carriages and men on horseback or elevated on buckets or boxes or suchlike, on tiptoes, craning their necks.

A ripple went from front to back of the whole assemblage and somebody shouted 'Here they come!'.

They were a sight to behold. The huge hairy man with the black hood over his head; the mouth, the nose, the gleaming eyes were all that were revealed. And the other man with the long legs and the long yellow hair and the long flowing moustaches which made him look like various statemen, generals and gunfighters. But Whip Delune did not need diplomacy, a quality of leadership or speed with firearms. All he needed was his fists and they were formidable. The Bear's balled hands were no bigger.

They were at it almost immediately, amid roars from the onlookers, all with a nice edge on them now.

The fight was one that would be remembered for a long time to come—but for a different reason to what might have been expected . . .

      *   *   *

She was bold in the way that she used to be. And so be

it, she thought.

She was not the sort to sneak in the night. She was what she was. Had she ever thought that, deep down, she would ever be any different? She loved greatly life and love. Could she settle for the rest of her days to being a rancher's wife, no matter how greatly prosperous? Could Lemmy Spring who was now Caleb Summer settle for such a life also? Was his dream of power and wealth a delusion that would ultimately destroy him? Was her dream of warmth and security merely an illusion?

She had been bitter—now, suddenly, she was elated. Her pulses raced at the thought of being with Amos Crowle again.

Was this the beginning of the end or the beginning of a new beginning?

She realised she did not care one way or the other.

She did not know where her husband was now. She had left her son in bed with Ma Berghof to watch over him. But it was as if the ranch, the family, back there in the night was part of another life. She had been living for the future. But now she was living for the present, the vital *now*, the way she used to do.

She asked the desk clerk the number of Amos Crowle's room. He was a youth she did not know and maybe he did not know her either. He told her the number and said that, as far as he knew, Mr Crowle was still up there.

She climbed the stairs. She had never been upstairs in this small hotel before, but she had seen so many staircases like it, so many passages, so many doors. And it was as if what had happened in between was only a dream.

She knocked on the door.

She heard him moving inside, the creak of floorboards, the soft *shushing* of feet. Amos had always moved like a cat.

The door opened and he stood there with his thumb hooked in his gunbelt. She knew that before he had opened the door and seen who it was his hand had been on the butt of his gun. She realised that his life, like the life of her husband, was one of eternal vigilance. Even Caleb's changed, scarred face had not changed him, this part of him, the vigilant gunfighter's caution, any more than it would have changed this man if he had had that operation, that mutilation.

But this man's face had not changed, nor had those slate-grey eyes that seemed to look right through a person. But they warmed now and he smiled his thin, crooked smile beneath the black moustache.

"Hallo, Lola. C'mon in." He stepped aside and she went past him with a swing of her hips and he closed the door behind her.

When he turned away from the door she was facing him. She wore a simple white shirtwaist with a bit of lace at the neck and small pearl buttons which fastened all down the front. Her brown skirt was tight at her hips and waist but flared at the bottom like the skirt of a Mexican dancer. She wore soft hide shoes that were very much like cut-down riding boots with their high heels and patterns chased in white cord.

Her raven hair was down to her shoulders and, from beneath her olive brow, high and unwrinkled, her lustrous brown eyes appraised him boldly.

"You look good, Lola," he said. "You look mighty good."

"Thank you, kind sir," she replied mockingly. "You don't look so bad yourself." The interplay with a man like this, that was what she liked. There was always an element of danger.

He crossed the room and went past her and she revolved. He took off his gunbelt and hung it on the bedpost. The room was frugally-appointed but it was clean and neat. In a way Crowle matched it right now. His hair was slicked and he had on a clean checked shirt. He had obviously had a shave recently and she could smell lotion, or maybe it was pomade. It was almost as if he had been expecting her.

She was a little frightened that this might be so. But the fright exhilarated her. He was an arrogant man. She liked his arrogance.

He sat down on the edge of the bed and he raised his hand and crooked a finger and smiled. She moved slowly towards him and raised her own hand but did not stretch it out, being coquettish. He caught hold of it though, and he pulled her down beside him.

He let go of her hand then. He raised his own hand and with fingers that seemed surprisingly gentle began to undo the small pearl buttons down the front of her shirtwaist.

EIGHTEEN

Parley Master's father had been a gunfighter.

He had been a bounty-hunter and he never brought his man back alive. He had wandered the length and breadth of the West, trailing his wife and his only son behind him. After bearing Parley, his mother had not been able to have any more children. She was a frail, pretty woman from a good family, Southern aristocracy, who had run away with a Western man whom her folks called 'poor-white'. She had gone back West with her man, cutting herself off from her family.

She loved her handsome, dangerous gunfighting man to the point of slavery.

She doted on her only son also, however, and, pervosely, she did not want him to grow up to be like his father.

The boy took after his father though. He had different ideas to his mother. He was nine years old when his father taught him the use of guns.

They became rich and they settled in a big frame house and kept horses and the father went off from time to time on various commissions.

It was during this time that the boy, far more than his parents, got to know Amos Crowle.

Crowle lived with his woman (Parley learned later that she had not been his wife) at a neighbouring spread. They had a son too, though he was much younger than Parley and Parley did not get to know him well. Parley learned from his father that Crowle, though still a young man, had been a well-known lawman, a *pistolero* of note.

While his father was away on trips Parley often worked at Crowle's little ranch to earn himself extra pocket money. There was no friendship between the two families and, later, Parley wondered whether this was due to his father's brand of work. He liked Amos Crowle.

Amos was away on a beef-buying trip when an obscure type of fever was rife and this was contracted by both his wife and his son. When Amos returned, he had no family left. He sold the ranch and moved on. The boy Parley was sorry to see him go.

He learned later that Crowle had taken up law-dogging again.

The legend of Black Heart grew.

One day, when expected home, Parley's father did not return. It was weeks later, the wife beside herself with anxiety, that she and the boy learned that their breadwinner had been killed in a gunfight with two brothers called Mabley. The boy Parley was fourteen years old.

In a few years the mother deteriorated so fast that she finally had to be put in an institution. Parley Masters was sixteen when he began his wanderings, began to hire out his gun.

He had a long memory. He caught up with the brothers Mabley in a small town in New Mexico and he killed them both in a straight stand-up gunfight.

He met Amos Crowle briefly in Kansas and they had a drink together. But they were going in different directions, maybe in more ways than one. At that time they were both on the hunt—but Amos wore a badge.

That was the last time Parley had seen Amos until now. He did not know whether Amos had spotted him.

It was night and Parley had had no more instructions from Caleb Summer. He did not feel like going into town again, although some of the boys who were not on duty had gone there for a saloon visit and maybe to pick up a few girls.

While he was working, Parley never involved himself with any particular female. He did not have a girl in this territory.

That evening he played desultory poker with some of the boys in the bunkhouse who, though like him off-duty, did not feel like visiting anyplace.

*   *   *

Hardneck Gordino lay on his bed of pain.

It was late at night but he was not sleeping.

He was no longer Bruno, the Hooded Bear, but just a fighter who had gotten hurt and would have to rest up for a while.

Hardneck had a white bandage around his head and his eyes looked cloudy. His wife, Oggie, sat at his bedside. But Hardneck the Bear, hooded or not, prizefighter or not, had not been laid up by any human agency, not even by such a ball of fire as Whip Delune.

Hardneck had been kicked in the head by a horse.

The arena in which the Bear-Whip prizefight had been staged was a small corral belonging to a horse ranch. Fractious broncs were kept in this corral, one at a time, thus separating them from the beasts in the larger corral and out on the range.

Before the small corral was cleared and swept in time for the fight it had been occupied by a real killer, a black and white stallion that not one of the ranch's premier riders had been able to break. Some careless ranny had put this ruffian in the big corral with the other horses and he hadn't liked this one little bit. Evidently he was strictly a loner.

He was a fighter too, and he had more going for him even than the two humans had who were now using his old home as an arena. It appeared he had gotten quite attached to that small corral. He might even have gotten to like the humans who came in from time to time and tried to ride him and eventually grown into a prime saddle horse for one of them.

None of the horses liked the people who milled around shouting. All the beasts were semi-wild, being newly broken and not ridden much yet, many of them awaiting sale. They had never seen so many people before or heard so much noise. But it was the black and white stallion who was enraged the most—he was not even frightened. Those humans were hiding *his* corral even from his sight. He had the equipment with which to fight them, teeth, hooves, and he liked to fight.

He began by kicking violently at the rails of the big corral, screaming at the other beasts there until some of them joined in.

The fence had been built to withstand such an onslaught, though probably never one as violent as this. It was shattered piecemeal, until there was room for a horse to get through. And the stallion was the first out, making like an arrow for the backs of the vociferous humans who were clustered round the small corral.

The rest of the horses followed him. They were all enjoying themselves now. They had the wind in their nostrils, freedom in their eyes. Not until the last moment were the people aware of them.

They were knocked to all sides. The men, in the highest standards of Western chivalry, tried to save the women. There was a shouting, a squealing, a scrambling. A woman fell and was dragged clear, her skirts most indecorously raised. A poke bonnet was trampled upon. Later a horse was seen galloping with this torn and bed-raggled bonnet in his teeth. A man was bitten in the neck. Another was kicked in the backside as he turned to run—doubtless he had no lady to succour.

The horses, led by the black and white stallion, having broken out of the large corral broke into the small corral, and through it.

Whip and the Bear had moved apart. Whip was looking bemused. As he still wore his black hood, the Bear's expression was unreadable. But he was turning towards Oggie at the corral fence. Oggie left the fence and ran towards her husband. She did not see the black and white stallion looming behind her. There was too much noise, too much dust.

The Bear shouted at the woman, running towards her. Whip was at the hooded man's heels. Whip was shouting too.

The Bear reached Oggie, grabbed her, flung her to one side. The black and white horse reared above the giant hooded man, a strange creature indeed, human and yet not human.

The horse struck downwards and the creature collapsed beneath its hooves.

The beast thundered on as Oggie and Whip ran to the fallen man's side. The rest of the horses went around the little group. They crashed through the other side of the small corral and galloped off across the plains.

"Ad!" Oggie's voice was raised in a keening cry of anguish.

Whip removed the hood. The bearded man began to groan. Other people were coming forward. The real identity of Bruno, the Hooded Bear, was going to be revealed, but that did not matter much now. The bearded man's eyes fluttered.

"Oggie?"

"I'm here, Ad. Oh, thank God."

Tall Lincrane was coming forward, and Rammer, and Jacko Rooney, and old Brackburn.

The ancient ex-rustler, ex-wrangler, ex-Injun-fighter, and fighter-manager shouted authoritatively, "Keep back, folks. Keep back, for Pete's sake!"

Brainless, clucking, prying, braying jackasses!

NINETEEN

Lola said: "He didn't tell me anything. Why would he?"

Caleb said: "Why wouldn't he? But you were both too busy with other matters no doubt."

"You should not have sent me."

"Maybe you should not have gone."

"Maybe," she said. But she felt no remorse. She did not know what she did feel.

She did not feel anything much. Suddenly this man in front of her, this husband, this father of her child, was like a stranger to her; a stranger with a scarred face and mad, hot eyes and a harsh and jeering voice which seemed to be trying to goad her into saying something, doing something.

But was Caleb trying to whip himself into something?

A stab of fear went through her but was then as suddenly no more.

"Did you tell him things? Did you tell him who you are, what you are now?"

He knows what I am, she thought, Crowle—he knows the *real* me. Aloud, she said: "I didn't tell him anything. I don't think he knows anything."

The light seemed to go out of his eyes, so that they were as blank as glass. But still they seemed to look right through her. Without seeing her, though. What does he want, she thought, what does he really want?

"Go to bed," he said tonelessly.

Often he sat up late, and she always asked him the same thing. "Are you coming?"

"Don't worry about me," he said.

She lay awake for a while and he did not join her during that time. She went to sleep, and she must have slept heavily. It was a great bed. There was plenty of room. And Caleb was a catlike man.

There was another catlike man. And the two became jumbled in her sleeping mind, although they were moving in a sort of sinister cloud.

When she awoke the sun was streaking through the window. The place beside her was empty, but the whole bed was rumpled. She did not know whether Caleb had slept silently beside her in his catlike way or whether she herself had tossed and turned over the whole length and breadth of the huge, soft four-poster with its velvet curtains which she always had flung back.

But now it was as if the curtains were still drawn, for she did not see the sun, and a black cloud was part of her, part of her spirit and her mind. Something terrible is going to happen, she thought.

The cloud moved in her mind like black smoke and a

great lethargy held her limbs . . .

*   *   *

When Parley Masters awoke, alarm coursing through him, it was to find his boss standing at the foot of the bed.

"Get up," said Caleb Summer. "We have things to do."

"It's early, isn't it?"

"It's late enough."

Caleb had awakened in his big armchair in the ranch-house. At first he had thought he was in bed, but a crick in his neck and a dullness in various limbs soon told him where he was. There was no dullness in his mind, however. His subconscious had worked out his problem for him while he slept and he knew now what he had to do.

Anyway, he figured it was the decision he would have had to make sooner or later, that was the way he was.

It was sort of inevitable.

Parley said: "Where are we going, boss?"

"We're going to town."

Night would have been better, Caleb thought. But this was something he did not want to do by night, this was something to be done in the daylight, do or die, survive or perish.

He would give himself an edge, that was all. Hell, what was he paying Parley for, anyway? It was time that young hellion earned his keep and proved that he was as good as he was supposed to be.

Nobody was going to shame Caleb Summer. And nobody was going to shame his woman. Even if he (Caleb) killed that woman afterwards.

*   *   *

It was true that Amos Crowle had not gotten any information from Lola Summer. He had previously learned who she was, but he had not told her that he knew. And she had not told him who she was. They had both played little games, and those little games had ended in the inevitable way.

It was something they would both remember. But it would not change things. Had either of them thought that it would? Amos Crowle did not hesitate in answering that question for himself.

For himself, the answer was No.

He had a way of talking to people, a subtle way of asking questions. But his manner could be authoritative or ruthless too. Like a drummer selling his wares, he sort of cut his cloth to suit his customer.

He had learned that Caleb Summer ran a spread called the Rainbow not far out of town. He learned that Caleb had a wife called Lola and they had a small son. Feelings in town about Caleb Summer were kind of mixed. He was not liked, but nobody seemed to know why. Seemed like he was the sort of man who was overly ambitious.

And there was the look of that scarred face of his'n, and those peculiar eyes!

Crowle had only been in town a short while when he

met the girl he had known as Lola Canalete in May and
Kate's Sunflower House in Abilene. It had not been
hard to discover that Lola Canalete was now Lola
Summer. What could a beautiful woman like that see in
a ghoul like Summer, the townsfolk wanted to know?
Crowle could have told them that Summer had not
always been a ghoul. Not physically anyway. But,
sardonically, he did not tell them anything.

He wondered whether Lola had told her husband
that she had seen him, Crowle. When she came to him
that night he wondered again, even though he had half-
expected her. Hell, women were strange cattle!
Specially a woman like that one . . .

I'll go out there in the morning, he thought, I'll have
the end of it.

He did not know that the Fates had a surprise in store
for him.

It was a long trip he had made. And all, indirectly, on
behalf of his friend, Hardneck Gordino. But the hunt
had become the whole, as it always did, and he had only
had fleeting thoughts of the big blackbearded giant
who, as far as he knew, still languished in a cell back in
the town of Lazy Bend in New Mexico.

Hardneck, caged like an animal. Like a big bear. I
ought to get back there, thought Crowle now, I ought to
get back there as soon as I can.

That morning he got up early and went downstairs.
There was nobody behind the desk in the lobby. He
figured it was too early for breakfast. Maybe he did not
need breakfast. Maybe he could get some early coffee in

one of the *cantinas* on the edge of town. These small towns deep in Texas usually had their *cantinas*. But he wanted to get going anyway. He hoped there was somebody at the stables so he could get his horse.

He walked out into the street. As he stepped off the boardwalk, the pocked and rutted higgledy-piggledy thoroughfare was deserted.

Then he saw two horses at the hitching rack along by the saloon.

He figured that the saloon would not be open yet. Maybe some dusty jaspers were so thirsty they were willing to wait awhile. Two new-come saddle-tramps probably.

Then the two men came out of the shadows by the saloon batwings and a little warning bell tinkled in the back of Crowle's head.

Some kind of a set-up?

But maybe he was being over-cautious.

But then one of the men, walking more quickly than his companion and with a sort of catlike lope, moved over to the other side of the narrow street. And the second man, younger, leaner, moved further out too, and a stab of recognition went through Crowle at the look of this one.

Then this younger one was facing him directly and was saying loudly, "We're calling you, Amos."

The street was empty. The morning sun struck obliquely across the hard-baked, pocked and rutted mud. They faced each other, the three of them, and neither of them had the sun in his eyes.

"Parley Masters," said Crowle, but so softly that neither of the other two could have heard him.

The other man had a face that Crowle did not recognise, a scarred, still, strange face. But there were the strange eyes too, and something about the way the man held himself, the way he moved, the whole *look* of him; those recognisable things.

"Mornin', Parley." Crowle had not known Parley was in town.

"Don't waste our time, Amos." Parley was still kind of shouting, a sort of cracked strain in his voice.

Crowle said: "You're calling me for this man, huh, Parley?"

"This is the man who has hired me. I always do what the man who's hired me tells me to do. He's the one who foots the bill."

"Do tell! Well, this one shouldn't need a hired gun. He should be able to do his own shooting—unless he's turned yellow, of course. This man might call himself Caleb Summer, but he's just the notorious Lemmy Spring with a new face. You've heard of Lemmy Spring, haven't you, Parley? You've heard of that stinking, back-shooting, yellow-bellied, ugly bastard. Can't you smell him, Parley? Don't you know a polecat when you get a smell of it?"

No, Parley had not known his boss's real identity, that was evident. He had not even suspected it. His arm, Parley's arm, which had been crooked, slowly dropped.

It was then that Caleb Summer went for his gun.

There was no jerkiness about it—it was all smooth speed.

Christ, he's fast, thought Crowle, and he was dropping to the ground. He was twisting himself sideways, too, all at the same time, to facilitate an easy drawing of his own special long-barrelled modified Dragoon Colt.

Summer's first shot kicked up the dust behind his target, having gone past Crowle and way above his head. Crowle thumbed the hammer of his own weapon and he heard Summers cry out. The man went backwards. And Parley Masters was moving too.

Parley had his gun lifted. It almost seemed that he had hesitated. He shouldn't have! Crowle, aiming deliberately, shot him in the shoulder, his right shoulder, destroying his gun arm.

Parley's heavy weapon spiralled into the air, came down. When it hit the ground it went off, the slug whining away harmlessly into nothingness. Parley staggered, then crumpled up. He lay on his side, his legs curled up, and Crowle heard him give deep, sobbing breaths.

Summer was on his feet. He was running. He was hugging himself. He was still as fast as quicksilver, although he was hurt. He reached his horse and was sheltered behind it. He still had his gun and he was firing recklessly as he hauled himself into the saddle. Crowle launched himself upwards, scuttled crablike onto the boardwalk and partial cover. But Summer did not come out, rode away from him, crouched over the saddle.

Crowle raised his gun level, then lowered it again. It was not a good shot. He ran forward and vaulted into the saddle of the other horse, Parley's mount.

People were coming into the street. Crowle pointed at Parley, yelled, "Take care of him."

He heard Parley call after him in a scream, "God damn you, Amos, I'll kill you for this. I'll kill you!"

TWENTY

Parley's horse was a good one. But Summer had a good mount, too, and it was heading for home.

The man was very low over the saddle, almost seemed to be hugging the horse's neck. He was certainly giving the beast its head.

Crowle saw the ranch-buildings, a cluster of them, neat in the morning sun.

There did not seem to be anybody about. All this that had happened seemed to be taking part in quietness, in loneliness. But back there in the town the gunshots had echoed along the street, and the whining shots had been like screams. Now there was only the soft thudding of horses' hooves and no wind and even the sun, as yet, had a benign touch about it.

The rider in front must have steered his horse away from a direct line to the buildings. Or maybe the beast always went that way. He carried his master into what looked like a small corral, although there were a few outhouses in and around there too.

Both horse and rider were obscured from Crowle's view for a moment of time.

But then, when he saw the horse again, its saddle was empty.

Crowle lowered himself in his own saddle, curled himself around and over the horse's barrel-body, Indian-fashion. Maybe Summer had actually fallen off his mount, was finished. But Crowle was taking no chances. If Summer had run, he had run because he hoped to fight again, and from a more strategic position maybe. Crowle knew the man was hit. Somehow, you always had the certainty of this; you knew it. If Summer had hit Crowle, he would have known it. You knew when you had got your man. In a close-to, straight stand-up gunfight like that, if you were any good at all you hit what you were aiming at—unless your opponent was mighty good too and moved like quicksilver.

Summer was good. But he had been hit. Trouble was, Crowle did not know how badly the man had been hit. Maybe after all it was not a bad one and Summer had been foxing and now thought he had Crowle where he wanted him.

Crowle did not ride straight for the outbuildings but steered his horse—Parley's horse, actually—in a sort of loop.

He kept his position so that his body was protected from shots if they came from that direction. His head was not such a big target, less so when he took off his hat and hung it on the saddle horn.

He drew his gun. "Go, boy!" The horse's hooves thudded rapidly, harshly against the ground and the man was swung and jolted in his precarious position.

"Go, boy!"

They did not go through the fences but around them. A rifle cracked spitefully but Crowle had not heard the slug. He only knew that Summer was still functioning, had picked his spot, was using his long gun.

Crowle kept riding. He made a circuit of the out-buildings, and then a half-circle. Two more shots were flung at him, but evidently Summer was not well-orientated. Crowle rode hard for the side of the buildings, leapt from his horse and, with a smart slap on its flank, sent the beast galloping on another ragged circuit.

He crouched against the wall. He heard Summer move on the other side of the split woods that made up the walls of this small feed barn. Summer was following the sound of the hoofbeats. And now the horse was going away.

Running on his tiptoes, Crowle moved to the corner, turned it. And that was when Summer showed himself at the door.

Crowle gave a shrill whistle and Summer swung around, the rifle lifting. Holding the gun at the end of his outstretched arm, the long barrel pointing like a finger, Crowle thumbed the hammer twice. The heavy gun bucked in his hand, the barrel jerking upwards functionally, twice. But the heavy bullets were sped on their way. And they both found their targets in the broadness of Summer's upper body.

The Winchester that Summer had been gripping flew out of his hand and hit the hard earth. The man was knocked backwards by the heavy slugs and he disappeared from view.

Crowle moved along, went through the narrow door which was now open wide.

Summer lay on his back. His eyes were wide and staring but there was no wild light in them now. That light had already died completely and the scarred face was set in a grimace, almost as if the once-handsome Lemmy Spring was laughing sardonically at what had come about. Crowle felt like telling him that it would have had to happen some day. But Lemmy would not have heard him.

One bullet had hit Summer squarely in the chest. Whether it was the first one or the second Crowle did not know, but it alone must have killed the man instantly, tearing through flesh and bone and vessels and, judging by the blood that was already seeping from beneath the body, making a terrible hole in the back as it ripped itself free. Blood spreads so quickly, thought Crowle dully. And he didn't think he would ever get used to seeing what terrible things a heavy fourty-four or forty-five calibre slug could do to the human frame.

The other bullet had entered the body at a more oblique angle and had possibly been deflected by the man's ribs. Summer had a third wound down by his hip, the one he had sustained back in the little cowtown, the name of which Crowle did not know. The blood had already been caked on this by the sun.

Crowle turned away from the body. He began to walk through the small corral. The horse, after having his small fling on his lonesome, was waiting for him at the other side.

Parley's horse, thought Crowle, a good beast, maybe an improvement on the one that Crowle had ridden to this territory. He was changing his horses a lot on this trip, but did not feel like returning this one to Parley. Parley would be all right. He might not be able to use his shooting arm again. Maybe he had the luck, thought Crowle sardonically. He'd live.

Lola came obliquely across the corral. She seemed to have appeared from nowhere. She walked like a somnambulist.

"I'm sorry, Lola," Crowle said.

She walked past him as if she had not heard him, as if she did not even see him.

Men were appearing but they were a distance away. A little boy in a small red dressing gown ran from the ranchhouse and across the sod calling, 'Mama!'

Crowle got on his horse and rode away.

*　　*　　*

"He ain't here, Mister Crowle," said Sheriff Ep Leary of Lazy Bend. "He busted out. Leastways, he was busted out by that old sidekick o' his, Brackburn. They've gone. Hardneck, his missus, Brackburn. The ranchhouse is empty. I got a posse after them." He did not tell Crowle anything about the 'posse'. "They had a big start. We lost 'em. I guess they're way out of my jurisdiction now."

Crowle did not stay in town long. He was soon on the trail again. He was beginning to feel like a goddam shuttlecock.

* * *

Hardneck was mending fine. The bandage had been taken off his head and now he only wore a plaster on the place where the horse had kicked him. Oggie and he were now resting-up, together with the rest of Jacko Rooney's Fight-to-a-Finish Brigade, in a little town not far from the horse ranch where the big bearded bruiser had almost gotten his cumuppance from the black and white stallion. And, although most of the horses had been rounded up, that one was still free.

The local doc had told Hardneck that he wouldn't be fighting again for quite a while, unless he wanted his fool brains addled completely.

Hardneck had said he didn't much feel like fighting.

Oggie had said that maybe this was a sort of judgment on them.

Hardneck hadn't known what she meant, still didn't.

It was a quiet time, a resting time.

But then, suddenly, things began to happen, things began to speed up like a rodeo bucker with firecrackers going off under his tail.

First of all, Amos Crowle turned up.

But Amos had mighty good news. Hardneck and his cohorts (that was what Amos called them) were in the clear now and could return home. Amos did not tell them the full story right away but Hardneck knew he would get around to it sooner or later, in his own good time.

Amos said it had taken him a helluva time to find them, Hardneck and his goddam Hooded Bear!

Oggie and Hardneck and Brackburn began to get ready to move. Oggie was in a sort of seventh heaven and Hardneck realised how hard it must have been for her to leave her home in the first place.

In the noontime Amos went for a drink with Tall Lincrane, Rammer, and Jacko Rooney. These three were all old acquaintances of the famous lawman.

Hardneck and Brackburn said they would join them later.

They were later, though, than they had intended to be and, as they approached the saloon, their four friends were coming out through the batwings and Crowle was in the forefront.

And that was when the lean young man with one arm in a sling and the other holding a shotgun with the butt balanced on his hip stepped out into the middle of the street and screamed 'Amos!'

Moving with silent stealth on his unusually small feet, Hardneck Gordino trotted up behind the younker and cold-cocked him with the butt of a forty-five.

"It's Parley Masters," said Crowle. "An old friend . . . But I busted his arm."

Now he had a cracked head too.

But that got better.

And when Oggie, Brackburn and Hardneck left for home, Parley went with them.

Crowle stayed behind. He didn't know whether Parley would ever forgive him